The House of Dust

Conrad Aiken

Contents

THE HOUSE OF DUST

BY

Conrad Aiken

THE HOUSE OF DUST

A Symphony

By Conrad Aiken

To Jessie

NOTE

. . . Parts of this poem have been printed in "The North American Review, Others, Poetry, Youth, Coterie, The Yale Review". . . . I am indebted to Lafcadio Hearn for the episode called "The Screen Maiden" in Part II.

THE HOUSE OF DUST

PART I.

I.

The sun goes down in a cold pale flare of light.
The trees grow dark: the shadows lean to the east:
And lights wink out through the windows, one by one.
A clamor of frosty sirens mourns at the night.
Pale slate-grey clouds whirl up from the sunken sun.

And the wandering one, the inquisitive dreamer of dreams,
The eternal asker of answers, stands in the street,
And lifts his palms for the first cold ghost of rain.
The purple lights leap down the hill before him.
The gorgeous night has begun again.

'I will ask them all, I will ask them all their dreams,
I will hold my light above them and seek their faces.
I will hear them whisper, invisible in their veins . . .'
The eternal asker of answers becomes as the darkness,
Or as a wind blown over a myriad forest,

Or as the numberless voices of long-drawn rains.

We hear him and take him among us, like a wind of music,
Like the ghost of a music we have somewhere heard;
We crowd through the streets in a dazzle of pallid lamplight,
We pour in a sinister wave, ascend a stair,
With laughter and cry, and word upon murmured word;
We flow, we descend, we turn . . . and the eternal dreamer
Moves among us like light, like evening air . . .

Good-night! Good-night! Good-night! We go our ways,
The rain runs over the pavement before our feet,
The cold rain falls, the rain sings.
We walk, we run, we ride. We turn our faces
To what the eternal evening brings.

Our hands are hot and raw with the stones we have laid,
We have built a tower of stone high into the sky,
We have built a city of towers.

Our hands are light, they are singing with emptiness.
Our souls are light; they have shaken a burden of hours . . .
What did we build it for? Was it all a dream? . . .
Ghostly above us in lamplight the towers gleam . . .
And after a while they will fall to dust and rain;
Or else we will tear them down with impatient hands;
And hew rock out of the earth, and build them again.

II.

One, from his high bright window in a tower,
Leans out, as evening falls,

And sees the advancing curtain of the shower
Splashing its silver on roofs and walls:
Sees how, swift as a shadow, it crosses the city,
And murmurs beyond far walls to the sea,
Leaving a glimmer of water in the dark canyons,
And silver falling from eave and tree.

One, from his high bright window, looking down,
Peers like a dreamer over the rain-bright town,
And thinks its towers are like a dream.
The western windows flame in the sun's last flare,
Pale roofs begin to gleam.

Looking down from a window high in a wall
He sees us all;
Lifting our pallid faces towards the rain,
Searching the sky, and going our ways again,
Standing in doorways, waiting under the trees . . .
There, in the high bright window he dreams, and sees
What we are blind to,--we who mass and crowd
From wall to wall in the darkening of a cloud.

The gulls drift slowly above the city of towers,
Over the roofs to the darkening sea they fly;
Night falls swiftly on an evening of rain.
The yellow lamps wink one by one again.
The towers reach higher and blacker against the sky.

III.

One, where the pale sea foamed at the yellow sand,
With wave upon slowly shattering wave,

Turned to the city of towers as evening fell;
And slowly walked by the darkening road toward it;
And saw how the towers darkened against the sky;
And across the distance heard the toll of a bell.

Along the darkening road he hurried alone,
With his eyes cast down,
And thought how the streets were hoarse with a tide of people,
With clamor of voices, and numberless faces . . .
And it seemed to him, of a sudden, that he would drown
Here in the quiet of evening air,
These empty and voiceless places . . .
And he hurried towards the city, to enter there.

Along the darkening road, between tall trees
That made a sinister whisper, loudly he walked.
Behind him, sea-gulls dipped over long grey seas.
Before him, numberless lovers smiled and talked.
And death was observed with sudden cries,
And birth with laughter and pain.
And the trees grew taller and blacker against the skies
And night came down again.

IV.

Up high black walls, up sombre terraces,
Clinging like luminous birds to the sides of cliffs,
The yellow lights went climbing towards the sky.
From high black walls, gleaming vaguely with rain,
Each yellow light looked down like a golden eye.

They trembled from coign to coign, and tower to tower,

Along high terraces quicker than dream they flew.
And some of them steadily glowed, and some soon vanished,
And some strange shadows threw.

And behind them all the ghosts of thoughts went moving,
Restlessly moving in each lamplit room,
From chair to mirror, from mirror to fire;
From some, the light was scarcely more than a gloom:
From some, a dazzling desire.

And there was one, beneath black eaves, who thought,
Combing with lifted arms her golden hair,
Of the lover who hurried towards her through the night;
And there was one who dreamed of a sudden death
As she blew out her light.

And there was one who turned from clamoring streets,
And walked in lamplit gardens among black trees,
And looked at the windy sky,
And thought with terror how stones and roots would freeze
And birds in the dead boughs cry . . .

And she hurried back, as snow fell, mixed with rain,
To mingle among the crowds again,
To jostle beneath blue lamps along the street;
And lost herself in the warm bright coiling dream,
With a sound of murmuring voices and shuffling feet.

And one, from his high bright window looking down
On luminous chasms that cleft the basalt town,
Hearing a sea-like murmur rise,
Desired to leave his dream, descend from the tower,
And drown in waves of shouts and laughter and cries.

V.

The snow floats down upon us, mingled with rain . . .
It eddies around pale lilac lamps, and falls
Down golden-windowed walls.
We were all born of flesh, in a flare of pain,
We do not remember the red roots whence we rose,
But we know that we rose and walked, that after a while
We shall lie down again.

The snow floats down upon us, we turn, we turn,
Through gorges filled with light we sound and flow . . .
One is struck down and hurt, we crowd about him,
We bear him away, gaze after his listless body;
But whether he lives or dies we do not know.

One of us sings in the street, and we listen to him;
The words ring over us like vague bells of sorrow.
He sings of a house he lived in long ago.
It is strange; this house of dust was the house I lived in;
The house you lived in, the house that all of us know.
And coiling slowly about him, and laughing at him,
And throwing him pennies, we bear away
A mournful echo of other times and places,
And follow a dream . . . a dream that will not stay.

Down long broad flights of lamplit stairs we flow;
Noisy, in scattered waves, crowding and shouting;
In broken slow cascades.
The gardens extend before us . . . We spread out swiftly;
Trees are above us, and darkness. The canyon fades . . .

And we recall, with a gleaming stab of sadness,
Vaguely and incoherently, some dream
Of a world we came from, a world of sun-blue hills . . .
A black wood whispers around us, green eyes gleam;
Someone cries in the forest, and someone kills.

We flow to the east, to the white-lined shivering sea;
We reach to the west, where the whirling sun went down;
We close our eyes to music in bright cafees.
We diverge from clamorous streets to streets that are silent.
We loaf where the wind-spilled fountain plays.

And, growing tired, we turn aside at last,
Remember our secret selves, seek out our towers,
Lay weary hands on the banisters, and climb;
Climbing, each, to his little four-square dream
Of love or lust or beauty or death or crime.

VI.

Over the darkened city, the city of towers,
The city of a thousand gates,
Over the gleaming terraced roofs, the huddled towers,
Over a somnolent whisper of loves and hates,
The slow wind flows, drearily streams and falls,
With a mournful sound down rain-dark walls.
On one side purples the lustrous dusk of the sea,
And dreams in white at the city's feet;
On one side sleep the plains, with heaped-up hills.
Oaks and beeches whisper in rings about it.
Above the trees are towers where dread bells beat.

The fisherman draws his streaming net from the sea
And sails toward the far-off city, that seems
Like one vague tower.
The dark bow plunges to foam on blue-black waves,
And shrill rain seethes like a ghostly music about him
In a quiet shower.

Rain with a shrill sings on the lapsing waves;
Rain thrills over the roofs again;
Like a shadow of shifting silver it crosses the city;
The lamps in the streets are streamed with rain;
And sparrows complain beneath deep eaves,
And among whirled leaves
The sea-gulls, blowing from tower to lower tower,
From wall to remoter wall,
Skim with the driven rain to the rising sea-sound
And close grey wings and fall . . .

. . . Hearing great rain above me, I now remember
A girl who stood by the door and shut her eyes:
Her pale cheeks glistened with rain, she stood and shivered.
Into a forest of silver she vanished slowly . . .
Voices about me rise . . .

Voices clear and silvery, voices of raindrops,--
'We struck with silver claws, we struck her down.
We are the ghosts of the singing furies . . . '
A chorus of elfin voices blowing about me
Weaves to a babel of sound. Each cries a secret.
I run among them, reach out vain hands, and drown.

'I am the one who stood beside you and smiled,

Thinking your face so strangely young . . . '
'I am the one who loved you but did not dare.'
'I am the one you followed through crowded streets,
The one who escaped you, the one with red-gleamed hair.'

'I am the one you saw to-day, who fell
Senseless before you, hearing a certain bell:
A bell that broke great memories in my brain.'
'I am the one who passed unnoticed before you,
Invisible, in a cloud of secret pain.'

'I am the one who suddenly cried, beholding
The face of a certain man on the dazzling screen.
They wrote me that he was dead. It was long ago.
I walked in the streets for a long while, hearing nothing,
And returned to see it again. And it was so.'

Weave, weave, weave, you streaks of rain!
I am dissolved and woven again . . .
Thousands of faces rise and vanish before me.
Thousands of voices weave in the rain.

'I am the one who rode beside you, blinking
At a dazzle of golden lights.
Tempests of music swept me: I was thinking
Of the gorgeous promise of certain nights:
Of the woman who suddenly smiled at me this day,
Smiled in a certain delicious sidelong way,
And turned, as she reached the door,
To smile once more . . .
Her hands are whiter than snow on midnight water.
Her throat is golden and full of golden laughter,

Her eyes are strange as the stealth of the moon
On a night in June . . .
She runs among whistling leaves; I hurry after;
She dances in dreams over white-waved water;
Her body is white and fragrant and cool,
Magnolia petals that float on a white-starred pool . . .
I have dreamed of her, dreaming for many nights
Of a broken music and golden lights,
Of broken webs of silver, heavily falling
Between my hands and their white desire:
And dark-leaved boughs, edged with a golden radiance,
Dipping to screen a fire . . .
I dream that I walk with her beneath high trees,
But as I lean to kiss her face,
She is blown aloft on wind, I catch at leaves,
And run in a moonless place;
And I hear a crashing of terrible rocks flung down,
And shattering trees and cracking walls,
And a net of intense white flame roars over the town,
And someone cries; and darkness falls . . .
But now she has leaned and smiled at me,
My veins are afire with music,
Her eyes have kissed me, my body is turned to light;
I shall dream to her secret heart tonight . . . '

He rises and moves away, he says no word,
He folds his evening paper and turns away;
I rush through the dark with rows of lamplit faces;
Fire bells peal, and some of us turn to listen,
And some sit motionless in their accustomed places.

Cold rain lashes the car-roof, scurries in gusts,
Streams down the windows in waves and ripples of lustre;

The lamps in the streets are distorted and strange.
Someone takes his watch from his pocket and yawns.
One peers out in the night for the place to change.

Rain . . . rain . . . rain . . . we are buried in rain,
It will rain forever, the swift wheels hiss through water,
Pale sheets of water gleam in the windy street.
The pealing of bells is lost in a drive of rain-drops.
Remote and hurried the great bells beat.

'I am the one whom life so shrewdly betrayed,
Misfortune dogs me, it always hunted me down.
And to-day the woman I love lies dead.
I gave her roses, a ring with opals;
These hands have touched her head.

'I bound her to me in all soft ways,
I bound her to me in a net of days,
Yet now she has gone in silence and said no word.
How can we face these dazzling things, I ask you?
There is no use: we cry: and are not heard.

'They cover a body with roses . . . I shall not see it . . .
Must one return to the lifeless walls of a city
Whose soul is charred by fire? . . . '
His eyes are closed, his lips press tightly together.
Wheels hiss beneath us. He yields us our desire.

'No, do not stare so--he is weak with grief,
He cannot face you, he turns his eyes aside;
He is confused with pain.
I suffered this. I know. It was long ago . . .
He closes his eyes and drowns in death again.'

The wind hurls blows at the rain-starred glistening windows,
The wind shrills down from the half-seen walls.
We flow on the mournful wind in a dream of dying;
And at last a silence falls.

VII.

Midnight; bells toll, and along the cloud-high towers
The golden lights go out . . .
The yellow windows darken, the shades are drawn,
In thousands of rooms we sleep, we await the dawn,
We lie face down, we dream,
We cry aloud with terror, half rise, or seem
To stare at the ceiling or walls . . .
Midnight . . . the last of shattering bell-notes falls.
A rush of silence whirls over the cloud-high towers,
A vortex of soundless hours.

'The bells have just struck twelve: I should be sleeping.
But I cannot delay any longer to write and tell you.
The woman is dead.
She died--you know the way. Just as we planned.
Smiling, with open sunlit eyes.
Smiling upon the outstretched fatal hand . . .'

He folds his letter, steps softly down the stairs.
The doors are closed and silent. A gas-jet flares.
His shadow disturbs a shadow of balustrades.
The door swings shut behind. Night roars above him.
Into the night he fades.

Wind; wind; wind; carving the walls;
Blowing the water that gleams in the street;
Blowing the rain, the sleet.
In the dark alley, an old tree cracks and falls,
Oak-boughs moan in the haunted air;
Lamps blow down with a crash and tinkle of glass . . .
Darkness whistles . . . Wild hours pass . . .

And those whom sleep eludes lie wide-eyed, hearing
Above their heads a goblin night go by;
Children are waked, and cry,
The young girl hears the roar in her sleep, and dreams
That her lover is caught in a burning tower,
She clutches the pillow, she gasps for breath, she screams . . .
And then by degrees her breath grows quiet and slow,
She dreams of an evening, long ago:
Of colored lanterns balancing under trees,
Some of them softly catching afire;
And beneath the lanterns a motionless face she sees,
Golden with lamplight, smiling, serene . . .
The leaves are a pale and glittering green,
The sound of horns blows over the trampled grass,
Shadows of dancers pass . . .
The face smiles closer to hers, she tries to lean
Backward, away, the eyes burn close and strange,
The face is beginning to change,--
It is her lover, she no longer desires to resist,
She is held and kissed.
She closes her eyes, and melts in a seethe of flame . . .
With a smoking ghost of shame . . .

Wind, wind, wind . . . Wind in an enormous brain
Blowing dark thoughts like fallen leaves . . .

The wind shrieks, the wind grieves;
It dashes the leaves on walls, it whirls then again;
And the enormous sleeper vaguely and stupidly dreams
And desires to stir, to resist a ghost of pain.

One, whom the city imprisoned because of his cunning,
Who dreamed for years in a tower,
Seizes this hour
Of tumult and wind. He files through the rusted bar,
Leans his face to the rain, laughs up at the night,
Slides down the knotted sheet, swings over the wall,
To fall to the street with a cat-like fall,
Slinks round a quavering rim of windy light,
And at last is gone,
Leaving his empty cell for the pallor of dawn . . .

The mother whose child was buried to-day
Turns her face to the window; her face is grey;
And all her body is cold with the coldness of rain.
He would have grown as easily as a tree,
He would have spread a pleasure of shade above her,
He would have been his father again . . .
His growth was ended by a freezing invisible shadow.
She lies, and does not move, and is stabbed by the rain.

Wind, wind, wind; we toss and dream;
We dream we are clouds and stars, blown in a stream:
Windows rattle above our beds;
We reach vague-gesturing hands, we lift our heads,
Hear sounds far off,--and dream, with quivering breath,
Our curious separate ways through life and death.

VIII.

The white fog creeps from the cold sea over the city,
Over the pale grey tumbled towers,--
And settles among the roofs, the pale grey walls.
Along damp sinuous streets it crawls,
Curls like a dream among the motionless trees
And seems to freeze.

The fog slips ghostlike into a thousand rooms,
Whirls over sleeping faces,
Spins in an atomy dance round misty street lamps;
And blows in cloudy waves over open spaces . . .

And one from his high window, looking down,
Peers at the cloud-white town,
And thinks its island towers are like a dream . . .
It seems an enormous sleeper, within whose brain
Laborious shadows revolve and break and gleam.

PART II.

I.

The round red sun heaves darkly out of the sea.
The walls and towers are warmed and gleam.
Sounds go drowsily up from streets and wharves.
The city stirs like one that is half in dream.

And the mist flows up by dazzling walls and windows,
Where one by one we wake and rise.
We gaze at the pale grey lustrous sea a moment,
We rub the darkness from our eyes,

And face our thousand devious secret mornings . . .
And do not see how the pale mist, slowly ascending,
Shaped by the sun, shines like a white-robed dreamer
Compassionate over our towers bending.

There, like one who gazes into a crystal,
He broods upon our city with sombre eyes;
He sees our secret fears vaguely unfolding,
Sees cloudy symbols shape to rise.

Each gleaming point of light is like a seed
Dilating swiftly to coiling fires.
Each cloud becomes a rapidly dimming face,
Each hurrying face records its strange desires.

We descend our separate stairs toward the day,
Merge in the somnolent mass that fills the street,
Lift our eyes to the soft blue space of sky,
And walk by the well-known walls with accustomed feet.

II. THE FULFILLED DREAM

More towers must yet be built--more towers destroyed--
Great rocks hoisted in air;
And he must seek his bread in high pale sunlight
With gulls about him, and clouds just over his eyes . . .
And so he did not mention his dream of falling

But drank his coffee in silence, and heard in his ears
That horrible whistle of wind, and felt his breath
Sucked out of him, and saw the tower flash by
And the small tree swell beneath him . . .
He patted his boy on the head, and kissed his wife,
Looked quickly around the room, to remember it,--
And so went out . . . For once, he forgot his pail.

Something had changed--but it was not the street--
The street was just the same--it was himself.
Puddles flashed in the sun. In the pawn-shop door
The same old black cat winked green amber eyes;
The butcher stood by his window tying his apron;
The same men walked beside him, smoking pipes,
Reading the morning paper . . .

He would not yield, he thought, and walk more slowly,
As if he knew for certain he walked to death:
But with his usual pace,--deliberate, firm,
Looking about him calmly, watching the world,
Taking his ease . . . Yet, when he thought again
Of the same dream, now dreamed three separate times,
Always the same, and heard that whistling wind,
And saw the windows flashing upward past him,--
He slowed his pace a little, and thought with horror
How monstrously that small tree thrust to meet him! . . .
He slowed his pace a little and remembered his wife.

Was forty, then, too old for work like this?
Why should it be? He'd never been afraid--
His eye was sure, his hand was steady . . .
But dreams had meanings.
He walked more slowly, and looked along the roofs,

All built by men, and saw the pale blue sky;
And suddenly he was dizzy with looking at it,
It seemed to whirl and swim,
It seemed the color of terror, of speed, of death . . .
He lowered his eyes to the stones, he walked more slowly;
His thoughts were blown and scattered like leaves;
He thought of the pail . . . Why, then, was it forgotten?
Because he would not need it?

Then, just as he was grouping his thoughts again
About that drug-store corner, under an arc-lamp,
Where first he met the girl whom he would marry,--
That blue-eyed innocent girl, in a soft blouse,--
He waved his hand for signal, and up he went
In the dusty chute that hugged the wall;
Above the tree; from girdered floor to floor;
Above the flattening roofs, until the sea
Lay wide and waved before him . . . And then he stepped
Giddily out, from that security,
To the red rib of iron against the sky,
And walked along it, feeling it sing and tremble;
And looking down one instant, saw the tree
Just as he dreamed it was; and looked away,
And up again, feeling his blood go wild.

He gave the signal; the long girder swung
Closer to him, dropped clanging into place,
Almost pushing him off. Pneumatic hammers
Began their madhouse clatter, the white-hot rivets
Were tossed from below and deftly caught in pails;
He signalled again, and wiped his mouth, and thought
A place so high in the air should be more quiet.
The tree, far down below, teased at his eyes,

Teased at the corners of them, until he looked,
And felt his body go suddenly small and light;
Felt his brain float off like a dwindling vapor;
And heard a whistle of wind, and saw a tree
Come plunging up to him, and thought to himself,
'By God--I'm done for now, the dream was right . . .'

III. INTERLUDE

The warm sun dreams in the dust, the warm sun falls
On bright red roofs and walls;
The trees in the park exhale a ghost of rain;
We go from door to door in the streets again,
Talking, laughing, dreaming, turning our faces,
Recalling other times and places . . .
We crowd, not knowing why, around a gate,
We crowd together and wait,
A stretcher is carried out, voices are stilled,
The ambulance drives away.
We watch its roof flash by, hear someone say
'A man fell off the building and was killed--
Fell right into a barrel . . .' We turn again
Among the frightened eyes of white-faced men,
And go our separate ways, each bearing with him
A thing he tries, but vainly, to forget,--
A sickened crowd, a stretcher red and wet.

A hurdy-gurdy sings in the crowded street,
The golden notes skip over the sunlit stones,
Wings are upon our feet.
The sun seems warmer, the winding street more bright,
Sparrows come whirring down in a cloud of light.

We bear our dreams among us, bear them all,
Like hurdy-gurdy music they rise and fall,
Climb to beauty and die.
The wandering lover dreams of his lover's mouth,
And smiles at the hostile sky.
The broker smokes his pipe, and sees a fortune.
The murderer hears a cry.

IV. NIGHTMARE

'Draw three cards, and I will tell your future . . .
Draw three cards, and lay them down,
Rest your palms upon them, stare at the crystal,
And think of time . . . My father was a clown,
My mother was a gypsy out of Egypt;
And she was gotten with child in a strange way;
And I was born in a cold eclipse of the moon,
With the future in my eyes as clear as day.'

I sit before the gold-embroidered curtain
And think her face is like a wrinkled desert.
The crystal burns in lamplight beneath my eyes.
A dragon slowly coils on the scaly curtain.
Upon a scarlet cloth a white skull lies.

'Your hand is on the hand that holds three lilies.
You will live long, love many times.
I see a dark girl here who once betrayed you.
I see a shadow of secret crimes.

'There was a man who came intent to kill you,
And hid behind a door and waited for you;

There was a woman who smiled at you and lied.
There was a golden girl who loved you, begged you,
Crawled after you, and died.

'There is a ghost of murder in your blood--
Coming or past, I know not which.
And here is danger--a woman with sea-green eyes,
And white-skinned as a witch . . .'

The words hiss into me, like raindrops falling
On sleepy fire . . . She smiles a meaning smile.
Suspicion eats my brain; I ask a question;
Something is creeping at me, something vile;

And suddenly on the wall behind her head
I see a monstrous shadow strike and spread,
The lamp puffs out, a great blow crashes down.
I plunge through the curtain, run through dark to the street,
And hear swift steps retreat . . .

The shades are drawn, the door is locked behind me.
Behind the door I hear a hammer sounding.
I walk in a cloud of wonder; I am glad.
I mingle among the crowds; my heart is pounding;
You do not guess the adventure I have had! . . .

Yet you, too, all have had your dark adventures,
Your sudden adventures, or strange, or sweet . . .
My peril goes out from me, is blown among you.
We loiter, dreaming together, along the street.

V. RETROSPECT

Round white clouds roll slowly above the housetops,
Over the clear red roofs they flow and pass.
A flock of pigeons rises with blue wings flashing,
Rises with whistle of wings, hovers an instant,
And settles slowly again on the tarnished grass.

And one old man looks down from a dusty window
And sees the pigeons circling about the fountain
And desires once more to walk among those trees.
Lovers walk in the noontime by that fountain.
Pigeons dip their beaks to drink from the water.
And soon the pond must freeze.

The light wind blows to his ears a sound of laughter,
Young men shuffle their feet, loaf in the sunlight;
A girl's laugh rings like a silver bell.
But clearer than all these sounds is a sound he hears
More in his secret heart than in his ears,--
A hammer's steady crescendo, like a knell.
He hears the snarl of pineboards under the plane,
The rhythmic saw, and then the hammer again,--
Playing with delicate strokes that sombre scale . . .
And the fountain dwindles, the sunlight seems to pale.

Time is a dream, he thinks, a destroying dream;
It lays great cities in dust, it fills the seas;
It covers the face of beauty, and tumbles walls.
Where was the woman he loved? Where was his youth?
Where was the dream that burned his brain like fire?
Even a dream grows grey at last and falls.

He opened his book once more, beside the window,
And read the printed words upon that page.
The sunlight touched his hand; his eyes moved slowly,
The quiet words enchanted time and age.

'Death is never an ending, death is a change;
Death is beautiful, for death is strange;
Death is one dream out of another flowing;
Death is a chorded music, softly going
By sweet transition from key to richer key.
Death is a meeting place of sea and sea.'

VI. ADELE AND DAVIS

She turned her head on the pillow, and cried once more.
And drawing a shaken breath, and closing her eyes,
To shut out, if she could, this dingy room,
The wigs and costumes scattered around the floor,--
Yellows and greens in the dark,--she walked again
Those nightmare streets which she had walked so often . . .
Here, at a certain corner, under an arc-lamp,
Blown by a bitter wind, she stopped and looked
In through the brilliant windows of a drug-store,
And wondered if she dared to ask for poison:
But it was late, few customers were there,
The eyes of all the clerks would freeze upon her,
And she would wilt, and cry . . . Here, by the river,
She listened to the water slapping the wall,
And felt queer fascination in its blackness:
But it was cold, the little waves looked cruel,
The stars were keen, and a windy dash of spray

Struck her cheek, and withered her veins . . . And so
She dragged herself once more to home, and bed.

Paul hadn't guessed it yet--though twice, already,
She'd fainted--once, the first time, on the stage.
So she must tell him soon--or else--get out . . .
How could she say it? That was the hideous thing.
She'd rather die than say it! . . . and all the trouble,
Months when she couldn't earn a cent, and then,
If he refused to marry her . . . well, what?
She saw him laughing, making a foolish joke,
His grey eyes turning quickly; and the words
Fled from her tongue . . . She saw him sitting silent,
Brooding over his morning coffee, maybe,
And tried again . . . she bit her lips, and trembled,
And looked away, and said . . . 'Say Paul, boy,--listen--
There's something I must tell you . . . ' There she stopped,
Wondering what he'd say . . . What would he say?
'Spring it, kid! Don't look so serious!'
'But what I've got to say--IS--serious!'
Then she could see how, suddenly, he would sober,
His eyes would darken, he'd look so terrifying--
He always did--and what could she do but cry?
Perhaps, then, he would guess--perhaps he wouldn't.
And if he didn't, but asked her 'What's the matter?'--
She knew she'd never tell--just say she was sick . . .
And after that, when would she dare again?
And what would he do--even suppose she told him?

If it were Felix! If it were only Felix!--
She wouldn't mind so much. But as it was,
Bitterness choked her, she had half a mind
To pay out Felix for never having liked her,

By making people think that it was he . . .
She'd write a letter to someone, before she died,--
Just saying 'Felix did it--and wouldn't marry.'
And then she'd die . . . But that was hard on Paul . . .
Paul would never forgive her--he'd never forgive her!
Sometimes she almost thought Paul really loved her . . .
She saw him look reproachfully at her coffin.

And then she closed her eyes and walked again
Those nightmare streets that she had walked so often:
Under an arc-lamp swinging in the wind
She stood, and stared in through a drug-store window,
Watching a clerk wrap up a little pill-box.
But it was late. No customers were there,--
Pitiless eyes would freeze her secret in her!
And then--what poison would she dare to ask for?
And if they asked her why, what would she say?

VII. TWO LOVERS: OVERTONES

Two lovers, here at the corner, by the steeple,
Two lovers blow together like music blowing:
And the crowd dissolves about them like a sea.
Recurring waves of sound break vaguely about them,
They drift from wall to wall, from tree to tree.
'Well, am I late?' Upward they look and laugh,
They look at the great clock's golden hands,
They laugh and talk, not knowing what they say:
Only, their words like music seem to play;
And seeming to walk, they tread strange sarabands.

'I brought you this . . . ' the soft words float like stars

Down the smooth heaven of her memory.
She stands again by a garden wall,
The peach tree is in bloom, pink blossoms fall,
Water sings from an opened tap, the bees
Glisten and murmur among the trees.
Someone calls from the house. She does not answer.
Backward she leans her head,
And dreamily smiles at the peach-tree leaves, wherethrough
She sees an infinite May sky spread
A vault profoundly blue.
The voice from the house fades far away,
The glistening leaves more vaguely ripple and sway . .
The tap is closed, the water ceases to hiss . . .
Silence . . . blue sky . . . and then, 'I brought you this . . . '
She turns again, and smiles . . . He does not know
She smiles from long ago . . .

She turns to him and smiles . . . Sunlight above him
Roars like a vast invisible sea,
Gold is beaten before him, shrill bells of silver;
He is released of weight, his body is free,
He lifts his arms to swim,
Dark years like sinister tides coil under him . . .
The lazy sea-waves crumble along the beach
With a whirring sound like wind in bells,
He lies outstretched on the yellow wind-worn sands
Reaching his lazy hands
Among the golden grains and sea-white shells . . .

'One white rose . . . or is it pink, to-day?'
They pause and smile, not caring what they say,
If only they may talk.
The crowd flows past them like dividing waters.

Dreaming they stand, dreaming they walk.

'Pink,--to-day!'--Face turns to dream-bright face,
Green leaves rise round them, sunshine settles upon them,
Water, in drops of silver, falls from the rose.
She smiles at a face that smiles through leaves from the mirror.
She breathes the fragrance; her dark eyes close . . .

Time is dissolved, it blows like a little dust:
Time, like a flurry of rain,
Patters and passes, starring the window-pane.
Once, long ago, one night,
She saw the lightning, with long blue quiver of light,
Ripping the darkness . . . and as she turned in terror
A soft face leaned above her, leaned softly down,
Softly around her a breath of roses was blown,
She sank in waves of quiet, she seemed to float
In a sea of silence . . . and soft steps grew remote . .

'Well, let us walk in the park . . . The sun is warm,
We'll sit on a bench and talk . . .' They turn and glide,
The crowd of faces wavers and breaks and flows.
'Look how the oak-tops turn to gold in the sunlight!
Look how the tower is changed and glows!'

Two lovers move in the crowd like a link of music,
We press upon them, we hold them, and let them pass;
A chord of music strikes us and straight we tremble;
We tremble like wind-blown grass.

What was this dream we had, a dream of music,
Music that rose from the opening earth like magic
And shook its beauty upon us and died away?

The long cold streets extend once more before us.
The red sun drops, the walls grow grey.

VIII. THE BOX WITH SILVER HANDLES

Well,--it was two days after my husband died--
Two days! And the earth still raw above him.
And I was sweeping the carpet in their hall.
In number four--the room with the red wall-paper--
Some chorus girls and men were singing that song
'They'll soon be lighting candles
Round a box with silver handles'--and hearing them sing it
I started to cry. Just then he came along
And stopped on the stairs and turned and looked at me,
And took the cigar from his mouth and sort of smiled
And said, 'Say, what's the matter?' and then came down
Where I was leaning against the wall,
And touched my shoulder, and put his arm around me . . .
And I was so sad, thinking about it,--
Thinking that it was raining, and a cold night,
With Jim so unaccustomed to being dead,--
That I was happy to have him sympathize,
To feel his arm, and leaned against him and cried.
And before I knew it, he got me into a room
Where a table was set, and no one there,
And sat me down on a sofa, and held me close,
And talked to me, telling me not to cry,
That it was all right, he'd look after me,--
But not to cry, my eyes were getting red,
Which didn't make me pretty. And he was so nice,
That when he turned my face between his hands,
And looked at me, with those blue eyes of his,

And smiled, and leaned, and kissed me--
Somehow I couldn't tell him not to do it,
Somehow I didn't mind, I let him kiss me,
And closed my eyes! . . . Well, that was how it started.
For when my heart was eased with crying, and grief
Had passed and left me quiet, somehow it seemed
As if it wasn't honest to change my mind,
To send him away, or say I hadn't meant it--
And, anyway, it seemed so hard to explain!
And so we sat and talked, not talking much,
But meaning as much in silence as in words,
There in that empty room with palms about us,
That private dining-room . . . And as we sat there
I felt my future changing, day by day,
With unknown streets opening left and right,
New streets with farther lights, new taller houses,
Doors swinging into hallways filled with light,
Half-opened luminous windows, with white curtains
Streaming out in the night, and sudden music,--
And thinking of this, and through it half remembering
A quick and horrible death, my husband's eyes,
The broken-plastered walls, my boy asleep,--
It seemed as if my brain would break in two.
My voice began to tremble . . . and when I stood,
And told him I must go, and said good-night--
I couldn't see the end. How would it end?
Would he return to-morrow? Or would he not?
And did I want him to--or would I rather
Look for another job?--He took my shoulders
Between his hands, and looked down into my eyes,
And smiled, and said good-night. If he had kissed me,
That would have--well, I don't know; but he didn't . .
And so I went downstairs, then, half elated,

Hoping to close the door before that party
In number four should sing that song again--
'They'll soon be lighting candles round a box with silver handles'--
And sure enough, I did. I faced the darkness.
And my eyes were filled with tears. And I was happy.

IX. INTERLUDE

The days, the nights, flow one by one above us,
The hours go silently over our lifted faces,
We are like dreamers who walk beneath a sea.
Beneath high walls we flow in the sun together.
We sleep, we wake, we laugh, we pursue, we flee.

We sit at tables and sip our morning coffee,
We read the papers for tales of lust or crime.
The door swings shut behind the latest comer.
We set our watches, regard the time.

What have we done? I close my eyes, remember
The great machine whose sinister brain before me
Smote and smote with a rhythmic beat.
My hands have torn down walls, the stone and plaster.
I dropped great beams to the dusty street.

My eyes are worn with measuring cloths of purple,
And golden cloths, and wavering cloths, and pale.
I dream of a crowd of faces, white with menace.
Hands reach up to tear me. My brain will fail.

Here, where the walls go down beneath our picks,
These walls whose windows gap against the sky,

Atom by atom of flesh and brain and marble
Will build a glittering tower before we die . . .

The young boy whistles, hurrying down the street,
The young girl hums beneath her breath.
One goes out to beauty, and does not know it.
And one goes out to death.

X. SUDDEN DEATH

'Number four--the girl who died on the table--
The girl with golden hair--'
The purpling body lies on the polished marble.
We open the throat, and lay the thyroid bare . . .

One, who held the ether-cone, remembers
Her dark blue frightened eyes.
He heard the sharp breath quiver, and saw her breast
More hurriedly fall and rise.
Her hands made futile gestures, she turned her head
Fighting for breath; her cheeks were flushed to scarlet,--
And, suddenly, she lay dead.

And all the dreams that hurried along her veins
Came to the darkness of a sudden wall.
Confusion ran among them, they whirled and clamored,
They fell, they rose, they struck, they shouted,
Till at last a pallor of silence hushed them all.

What was her name? Where had she walked that morning?
Through what dark forest came her feet?
Along what sunlit walls, what peopled street?

Backward he dreamed along a chain of days,
He saw her go her strange and secret ways,
Waking and sleeping, noon and night.
She sat by a mirror, braiding her golden hair.
She read a story by candlelight.

Her shadow ran before her along the street,
She walked with rhythmic feet,
Turned a corner, descended a stair.
She bought a paper, held it to scan the headlines,
Smiled for a moment at sea-gulls high in sunlight,
And drew deep breaths of air.

Days passed, bright clouds of days. Nights passed. And music
Murmured within the walls of lighted windows.
She lifted her face to the light and danced.
The dancers wreathed and grouped in moving patterns,
Clustered, receded, streamed, advanced.

Her dress was purple, her slippers were golden,
Her eyes were blue; and a purple orchid
Opened its golden heart on her breast . . .
She leaned to the surly languor of lazy music,
Leaned on her partner's arm to rest.
The violins were weaving a weft of silver,
The horns were weaving a lustrous brede of gold,
And time was caught in a glistening pattern,
Time, too elusive to hold . . .

Shadows of leaves fell over her face,--and sunlight:
She turned her face away.
Nearer she moved to a crouching darkness

With every step and day.

Death, who at first had thought of her only an instant,
At a great distance, across the night,
Smiled from a window upon her, and followed her slowly
From purple light to light.

Once, in her dreams, he spoke out clearly, crying,
'I am the murderer, death.
I am the lover who keeps his appointment
At the doors of breath!'

She rose and stared at her own reflection,
Half dreading there to find
The dark-eyed ghost, waiting beside her,
Or reaching from behind
To lay pale hands upon her shoulders . . .
Or was this in her mind? . . .

She combed her hair. The sunlight glimmered
Along the tossing strands.
Was there a stillness in this hair,--
A quiet in these hands?

Death was a dream. It could not change these eyes,
Blow out their light, or turn this mouth to dust.
She combed her hair and sang. She would live forever.
Leaves flew past her window along a gust . . .
And graves were dug in the earth, and coffins passed,
And music ebbed with the ebbing hours.
And dreams went along her veins, and scattering clouds
Threw streaming shadows on walls and towers.

XI.

Snow falls. The sky is grey, and sullenly glares
With purple lights in the canyoned street.
The fiery sign on the dark tower wreathes and flares . . .
The trodden grass in the park is covered with white,
The streets grow silent beneath our feet . . .
The city dreams, it forgets its past to-night.

And one, from his high bright window looking down
Over the enchanted whiteness of the town,
Seeing through whirls of white the vague grey towers,
Desires like this to forget what will not pass,
The littered papers, the dust, the tarnished grass,
Grey death, stale ugliness, and sodden hours.
Deep in his heart old bells are beaten again,
Slurred bells of grief and pain,
Dull echoes of hideous times and poisonous places.
He desires to drown in a cold white peace of snow.
He desires to forget a million faces . . .

In one room breathes a woman who dies of hunger.
The clock ticks slowly and stops. And no one winds it.
In one room fade grey violets in a vase.
Snow flakes faintly hiss and melt on the window.
In one room, minute by minute, the flutist plays
The lamplit page of music, the tireless scales.
His hands are trembling, his short breath fails.

In one room, silently, lover looks upon lover,
And thinks the air is fire.
The drunkard swears and touches the harlot's heartstrings

With the sudden hand of desire.

And one goes late in the streets, and thinks of murder;
And one lies staring, and thinks of death.
And one, who has suffered, clenches her hands despairing,
And holds her breath . . .

Who are all these, who flow in the veins of the city,
Coil and revolve and dream,
Vanish or gleam?
Some mount up to the brain and flower in fire.
Some are destroyed; some die; some slowly stream.

And the new are born who desire to destroy the old;
And fires are kindled and quenched; and dreams are broken,
And walls flung down . . .
And the slow night whirls in snow over towers of dreamers,
And whiteness hushes the town.

PART III

I

As evening falls,
And the yellow lights leap one by one
Along high walls;
And along black streets that glisten as if with rain,
The muted city seems
Like one in a restless sleep, who lies and dreams

Of vague desires, and memories, and half-forgotten pain . . .
Along dark veins, like lights the quick dreams run,
Flash, are extinguished, flash again,
To mingle and glow at last in the enormous brain
And die away . . .
As evening falls,
A dream dissolves these insubstantial walls,--
A myriad secretly gliding lights lie bare . . .
The lovers rise, the harlot combs her hair,
The dead man's face grows blue in the dizzy lamplight,
The watchman climbs the stair . . .
The bank defaulter leers at a chaos of figures,
And runs among them, and is beaten down;
The sick man coughs and hears the chisels ringing;
The tired clown
Sees the enormous crowd, a million faces,
Motionless in their places,
Ready to laugh, and seize, and crush and tear . . .
The dancer smooths her hair,
Laces her golden slippers, and runs through the door
To dance once more,
Hearing swift music like an enchantment rise,
Feeling the praise of a thousand eyes.

As darkness falls
The walls grow luminous and warm, the walls
Tremble and glow with the lives within them moving,
Moving like music, secret and rich and warm.
How shall we live tonight? Where shall we turn?
To what new light or darkness yearn?
A thousand winding stairs lead down before us;
And one by one in myriads we descend
By lamplit flowered walls, long balustrades,

Through half-lit halls which reach no end.

II. THE SCREEN MAIDEN

You read--what is it, then that you are reading?
What music moves so silently in your mind?
Your bright hand turns the page.
I watch you from my window, unsuspected:
You move in an alien land, a silent age . . .

. . . The poet--what was his name--? Tokkei--Tokkei--
The poet walked alone in a cold late rain,
And thought his grief was like the crying of sea-birds;
For his lover was dead, he never would love again.

Rain in the dreams of the mind--rain forever--
Rain in the sky of the heart--rain in the willows--
But then he saw this face, this face like flame,
This quiet lady, this portrait by Hiroshigi;
And took it home with him; and with it came

What unexpected changes, subtle as weather!
The dark room, cold as rain,
Grew faintly fragrant, stirred with a stir of April,
Warmed its corners with light again,

And smoke of incense whirled about this portrait,
And the quiet lady there,
So young, so quietly smiling, with calm hands,
Seemed ready to loose her hair,

And smile, and lean from the picture, or say one word,

The word already clear,
Which seemed to rise like light between her eyelids . .
He held his breath to hear,

And smiled for shame, and drank a cup of wine,
And held a candle, and searched her face
Through all the little shadows, to see what secret
Might give so warm a grace . . .

Was it the quiet mouth, restrained a little?
The eyes, half-turned aside?
The jade ring on her wrist, still almost swinging? . . .
The secret was denied,

He chose his favorite pen and drew these verses,
And slept; and as he slept
A dream came into his heart, his lover entered,
And chided him, and wept.

And in the morning, waking, he remembered,
And thought the dream was strange.
Why did his darkened lover rise from the garden?
He turned, and felt a change,

As if a someone hidden smiled and watched him . . .
Yet there was only sunlight there.
Until he saw those young eyes, quietly smiling,
And held his breath to stare,

And could have sworn her cheek had turned--a little . . .
Had slightly turned away . . .
Sunlight dozed on the floor . . . He sat and wondered,
Nor left his room that day.

And that day, and for many days thereafter,
He sat alone, and thought
No lady had ever lived so beautiful
As Hiroshigi wrought . . .

Or if she lived, no matter in what country,
By what far river or hill or lonely sea,
He would look in every face until he found her . . .
There was no other as fair as she.

And before her quiet face he burned soft incense,
And brought her every day
Boughs of the peach, or almond, or snow-white cherry,
And somehow, she seemed to say,

That silent lady, young, and quietly smiling,
That she was happy there;
And sometimes, seeing this, he started to tremble,
And desired to touch her hair,

To lay his palm along her hand, touch faintly
With delicate finger-tips
The ghostly smile that seemed to hover and vanish
Upon her lips . . .

Until he knew he loved this quiet lady;
And night by night a dread
Leered at his dreams, for he knew that Hiroshigi
Was many centuries dead,--

And the lady, too, was dead, and all who knew her . .
Dead, and long turned to dust . . .

The thin moon waxed and waned, and left him paler,
The peach leaves flew in a gust,

And he would surely have died; but there one day
A wise man, white with age,
Stared at the portrait, and said, 'This Hiroshigi
Knew more than archimage,--

Cunningly drew the body, and called the spirit,
Till partly it entered there . . .
Sometimes, at death, it entered the portrait wholly . .
Do all I say with care,

And she you love may come to you when you call her . . . '
So then this ghost, Tokkei,
Ran in the sun, bought wine of a hundred merchants,
And alone at the end of day

Entered the darkening room, and faced the portrait,
And saw the quiet eyes
Gleaming and young in the dusk, and held the wine-cup,
And knelt, and did not rise,

And said, aloud, 'Lo-san, will you drink this wine?'
Said it three times aloud.
And at the third the faint blue smoke of incense
Rose to the walls in a cloud,

And the lips moved faintly, and the eyes, and the calm hands stirred;
And suddenly, with a sigh,
The quiet lady came slowly down from the portrait,
And stood, while worlds went by,

And lifted her young white hands and took the wine cup;
And the poet trembled, and said,
'Lo-san, will you stay forever?'--'Yes, I will stay.'--
'But what when I am dead?'

'When you are dead your spirit will find my spirit,
And then we shall die no more.'
Music came down upon them, and spring returning,
They remembered worlds before,

And years went over the earth, and over the sea,
And lovers were born and spoke and died,
But forever in sunlight went these two immortal,
Tokkei and the quiet bride . . .

III. HAUNTED CHAMBERS

The lamplit page is turned, the dream forgotten;
The music changes tone, you wake, remember
Deep worlds you lived before,--deep worlds hereafter
Of leaf on falling leaf, music on music,
Rain and sorrow and wind and dust and laughter.

Helen was late and Miriam came too soon.
Joseph was dead, his wife and children starving.
Elaine was married and soon to have a child.
You dreamed last night of fiddler-crabs with fiddles;
They played a buzzing melody, and you smiled.

To-morrow--what? And what of yesterday?
Through soundless labyrinths of dream you pass,
Through many doors to the one door of all.

Soon as it's opened we shall hear a music:
Or see a skeleton fall . . .

We walk with you. Where is it that you lead us?
We climb the muffled stairs beneath high lanterns.
We descend again. We grope through darkened cells.
You say: this darkness, here, will slowly kill me.
It creeps and weighs upon me . . . Is full of bells.

This is the thing remembered I would forget--
No matter where I go, how soft I tread,
This windy gesture menaces me with death.
Fatigue! it says, and points its finger at me;
Touches my throat and stops my breath.

My fans--my jewels--the portrait of my husband--
The torn certificate for my daughter's grave--
These are but mortal seconds in immortal time.
They brush me, fade away: like drops of water.
They signify no crime.

Let us retrace our steps: I have deceived you:
Nothing is here I could not frankly tell you:
No hint of guilt, or faithlessness, or threat.
Dreams--they are madness. Staring eyes--illusion.
Let us return, hear music, and forget . . .

IV. ILLICIT

Of what she said to me that night--no matter.
The strange thing came next day.
My brain was full of music--something she played me--;

I couldn't remember it all, but phrases of it
Wreathed and wreathed among faint memories,
Seeking for something, trying to tell me something,
Urging to restlessness: verging on grief.
I tried to play the tune, from memory,--
But memory failed: the chords and discords climbed
And found no resolution--only hung there,
And left me morbid . . . Where, then, had I heard it? . . .
What secret dusty chamber was it hinting?
'Dust', it said, 'dust . . . and dust . . . and sunlight . .
A cold clear April evening . . . snow, bedraggled,
Rain-worn snow, dappling the hideous grass . . .
And someone walking alone; and someone saying
That all must end, for the time had come to go . . . '
These were the phrases . . . but behind, beneath them
A greater shadow moved: and in this shadow
I stood and guessed . . . Was it the blue-eyed lady?
The one who always danced in golden slippers--
And had I danced with her,--upon this music?
Or was it further back--the unplumbed twilight
Of childhood?--No--much recenter than that.

You know, without my telling you, how sometimes
A word or name eludes you, and you seek it
Through running ghosts of shadow,--leaping at it,
Lying in wait for it to spring upon it,
Spreading faint snares for it of sense or sound:
Until, of a sudden, as if in a phantom forest,
You hear it, see it flash among the branches,
And scarcely knowing how, suddenly have it--
Well, it was so I followed down this music,
Glimpsing a face in darkness, hearing a cry,
Remembering days forgotten, moods exhausted,

Corners in sunlight, puddles reflecting stars--;
Until, of a sudden, and least of all suspected,
The thing resolved itself: and I remembered
An April afternoon, eight years ago--
Or was it nine?--no matter--call it nine--
A room in which the last of sunlight faded;
A vase of violets, fragrance in white curtains;
And, she who played the same thing later, playing.

She played this tune. And in the middle of it
Abruptly broke it off, letting her hands
Fall in her lap. She sat there so a moment,
With shoulders drooped, then lifted up a rose,
One great white rose, wide opened like a lotos,
And pressed it to her cheek, and closed her eyes.

'You know--we've got to end this--Miriam loves you . . .
If she should ever know, or even guess it,--
What would she do?--Listen!--I'm not absurd . . .
I'm sure of it. If you had eyes, for women--
To understand them--which you've never had--
You'd know it too . . . ' So went this colloquy,
Half humorous, with undertones of pathos,
Half grave, half flippant . . . while her fingers, softly,
Felt for this tune, played it and let it fall,
Now note by singing note, now chord by chord,
Repeating phrases with a kind of pleasure . . .
Was it symbolic of the woman's weakness
That she could neither break it--nor conclude?
It paused . . . and wandered . . . paused again; while she,
Perplexed and tired, half told me I must go,--
Half asked me if I thought I ought to go . . .

Well, April passed with many other evenings,
Evenings like this, with later suns and warmer,
With violets always there, and fragrant curtains . . .
And she was right: and Miriam found it out . . .
And after that, when eight deep years had passed--
Or nine--we met once more,--by accident . . .
But was it just by accident, I wonder,
She played this tune?--Or what, then, was intended? . . .

V. MELODY IN A RESTAURANT

The cigarette-smoke loops and slides above us,
Dipping and swirling as the waiter passes;
You strike a match and stare upon the flame.
The tiny fire leaps in your eyes a moment,
And dwindles away as silently as it came.

This melody, you say, has certain voices--
They rise like nereids from a river, singing,
Lift white faces, and dive to darkness again.
Wherever you go you bear this river with you:
A leaf falls,--and it flows, and you have pain.

So says the tune to you--but what to me?
What to the waiter, as he pours your coffee,
The violinist who suavely draws his bow?
That man, who folds his paper, overhears it.
A thousand dreams revolve and fall and flow.

Some one there is who sees a virgin stepping
Down marble stairs to a deep tomb of roses:
At the last moment she lifts remembering eyes.

Green leaves blow down. The place is checked with shadows.
A long-drawn murmur of rain goes down the skies.
And oaks are stripped and bare, and smoke with lightning:
And clouds are blown and torn upon high forests,
And the great sea shakes its walls.
And then falls silence . . . And through long silence falls
This melody once more:
'Down endless stairs she goes, as once before.'

So says the tune to him--but what to me?
What are the worlds I see?
What shapes fantastic, terrible dreams? . . .
I go my secret way, down secret alleys;
My errand is not so simple as it seems.

VI. PORTRAIT OF ONE DEAD

This is the house. On one side there is darkness,
On one side there is light.
Into the darkness you may lift your lanterns--
O, any number--it will still be night.
And here are echoing stairs to lead you downward
To long sonorous halls.
And here is spring forever at these windows,
With roses on the walls.

This is her room. On one side there is music--
On one side not a sound.
At one step she could move from love to silence,
Feel myriad darkness coiling round.
And here are balconies from which she heard you,
Your steady footsteps on the stair.

And here the glass in which she saw your shadow
As she unbound her hair.

Here is the room--with ghostly walls dissolving--
The twilight room in which she called you 'lover';
And the floorless room in which she called you 'friend.'
So many times, in doubt, she ran between them!--
Through windy corridors of darkening end.

Here she could stand with one dim light above her
And hear far music, like a sea in caverns,
Murmur away at hollowed walls of stone.
And here, in a roofless room where it was raining,
She bore the patient sorrow of rain alone.

Your words were walls which suddenly froze around her.
Your words were windows,--large enough for moonlight,
Too small to let her through.
Your letters--fragrant cloisters faint with music.
The music that assuaged her there was you.

How many times she heard your step ascending
Yet never saw your face!
She heard them turn again, ring slowly fainter,
Till silence swept the place.
Why had you gone? . . . The door, perhaps, mistaken . . .
You would go elsewhere. The deep walls were shaken.

A certain rose-leaf--sent without intention--
Became, with time, a woven web of fire--
She wore it, and was warm.
A certain hurried glance, let fall at parting,
Became, with time, the flashings of a storm.

Yet, there was nothing asked, no hint to tell you
Of secret idols carved in secret chambers
From all you did and said.
Nothing was done, until at last she knew you.
Nothing was known, till, somehow, she was dead.

How did she die?--You say, she died of poison.
Simple and swift. And much to be regretted.
You did not see her pass
So many thousand times from light to darkness,
Pausing so many times before her glass;

You did not see how many times she hurried
To lean from certain windows, vainly hoping,
Passionate still for beauty, remembered spring.
You did not know how long she clung to music,
You did not hear her sing.

Did she, then, make the choice, and step out bravely
From sound to silence--close, herself, those windows?
Or was it true, instead,
That darkness moved,--for once,--and so possessed her? . . .
We'll never know, you say, for she is dead.

VII. PORCELAIN

You see that porcelain ranged there in the window--
Platters and soup-plates done with pale pink rosebuds,
And tiny violets, and wreaths of ivy?
See how the pattern clings to the gleaming edges!
They're works of art--minutely seen and felt,

Each petal done devoutly. Is it failure
To spend your blood like this?

Study them . . . you will see there, in the porcelain,
If you stare hard enough, a sort of swimming
Of lights and shadows, ghosts within a crystal--
My brain unfolding! There you'll see me sitting
Day after day, close to a certain window,
Looking down, sometimes, to see the people . . .

Sometimes my wife comes there to speak to me . . .
Sometimes the grey cat waves his tail around me . . .
Goldfish swim in a bowl, glisten in sunlight,
Dilate to a gorgeous size, blow delicate bubbles,
Drowse among dark green weeds. On rainy days,
You'll see a gas-light shedding light behind me--
An eye-shade round my forehead. There I sit,
Twirling the tiny brushes in my paint-cups,
Painting the pale pink rosebuds, minute violets,
Exquisite wreaths of dark green ivy leaves.
On this leaf, goes a dream I dreamed last night
Of two soft-patterned toads--I thought them stones,
Until they hopped! And then a great black spider,--
Tarantula, perhaps, a hideous thing,--
It crossed the room in one tremendous leap.
Here,--as I coil the stems between two leaves,--
It is as if, dwindling to atomy size,
I cried the secret between two universes . . .
A friend of mine took hasheesh once, and said
Just as he fell asleep he had a dream,--
Though with his eyes wide open,--
And felt, or saw, or knew himself a part
Of marvelous slowly-wreathing intricate patterns,

Plane upon plane, depth upon coiling depth,
Amazing leaves, folding one on another,
Voluted grasses, twists and curves and spirals--
All of it darkly moving . . . as for me,
I need no hasheesh for it--it's too easy!
Soon as I shut my eyes I set out walking
In a monstrous jungle of monstrous pale pink roseleaves,
Violets purple as death, dripping with water,
And ivy-leaves as big as clouds above me.

Here, in a simple pattern of separate violets--
With scalloped edges gilded--here you have me
Thinking of something else. My wife, you know,--
There's something lacking--force, or will, or passion,
I don't know what it is--and so, sometimes,
When I am tired, or haven't slept three nights,
Or it is cloudy, with low threat of rain,
I get uneasy--just like poplar trees
Ruffling their leaves--and I begin to think
Of poor Pauline, so many years ago,
And that delicious night. Where is she now?
I meant to write--but she has moved, by this time,
And then, besides, she might find out I'm married.
Well, there is more--I'm getting old and timid--
The years have gnawed my will. I've lost my nerve!
I never strike out boldly as I used to--
But sit here, painting violets, and remember
That thrilling night. Photographers, she said,
Asked her to pose for them; her eyes and forehead,--
Dark brown eyes, and a smooth and pallid forehead,--
Were thought so beautiful.--And so they were.
Pauline . . . These violets are like words remembered . . .
Darling! she whispered . . . Darling! . . . Darling! . . . Darling!

Well, I suppose such days can come but once.
Lord, how happy we were! . . .

Here, if you only knew it, is a story--
Here, in these leaves. I stopped my work to tell it,
And then, when I had finished, went on thinking:
A man I saw on a train . . . I was still a boy . . .
Who killed himself by diving against a wall.
Here is a recollection of my wife,
When she was still my sweetheart, years ago.
It's funny how things change,--just change, by growing,
Without an effort . . . And here are trivial things,--
A chill, an errand forgotten, a cut while shaving;
A friend of mine who tells me he is married . . .
Or is that last so trivial? Well, no matter!

This is the sort of thing you'll see of me,
If you look hard enough. This, in its way,
Is a kind of fame. My life arranged before you
In scrolls of leaves, rosebuds, violets, ivy,
Clustered or wreathed on plate and cup and platter . . .
Sometimes, I say, I'm just like John the Baptist--
You have my head before you . . . on a platter.

VIII. COFFINS: INTERLUDE

Wind blows. Snow falls. The great clock in its tower
Ticks with reverberant coil and tolls the hour:
At the deep sudden stroke the pigeons fly . . .
The fine snow flutes the cracks between the flagstones.
We close our coats, and hurry, and search the sky.

We are like music, each voice of it pursuing
A golden separate dream, remote, persistent,
Climbing to fire, receding to hoarse despair.
What do you whisper, brother? What do you tell me? . . .
We pass each other, are lost, and do not care.

One mounts up to beauty, serenely singing,
Forgetful of the steps that cry behind him;
One drifts slowly down from a waking dream.
One, foreseeing, lingers forever unmoving . . .
Upward and downward, past him there, we stream.

One has death in his eyes: and walks more slowly.
Death, among jonquils, told him a freezing secret.
A cloud blows over his eyes, he ponders earth.
He sees in the world a forest of sunlit jonquils:
A slow black poison huddles beneath that mirth.

Death, from street to alley, from door to window,
Cries out his news,--of unplumbed worlds approaching,
Of a cloud of darkness soon to destroy the tower.
But why comes death,--he asks,--in a world so perfect?
Or why the minute's grey in the golden hour?

Music, a sudden glissando, sinister, troubled,
A drift of wind-torn petals, before him passes
Down jangled streets, and dies.
The bodies of old and young, of maimed and lovely,
Are slowly borne to earth, with a dirge of cries.

Down cobbled streets they come; down huddled stairways;
Through silent halls; through carven golden doorways;
From freezing rooms as bare as rock.

The curtains are closed across deserted windows.
Earth streams out of the shovel; the pebbles knock.

Mary, whose hands rejoiced to move in sunlight;
Silent Elaine; grave Anne, who sang so clearly;
Fugitive Helen, who loved and walked alone;
Miriam too soon dead, darkly remembered;
Childless Ruth, who sorrowed, but could not atone;

Jean, whose laughter flashed over depths of terror,
And Eloise, who desired to love but dared not;
Doris, who turned alone to the dark and cried,--
They are blown away like windflung chords of music,
They drift away; the sudden music has died.

And one, with death in his eyes, comes walking slowly
And sees the shadow of death in many faces,
And thinks the world is strange.
He desires immortal music and spring forever,
And beauty that knows no change.

IX. CABARET

We sit together and talk, or smoke in silence.
You say (but use no words) 'this night is passing
As other nights when we are dead will pass . . .'
Perhaps I misconstrue you: you mean only,
'How deathly pale my face looks in that glass . . .'

You say: 'We sit and talk, of things important . . .
How many others like ourselves, this instant,
Mark the pendulum swinging against the wall?

How many others, laughing, sip their coffee--
Or stare at mirrors, and do not talk at all? . . .

'This is the moment' (so you would say, in silence)
When suddenly we have had too much of laughter:
And a freezing stillness falls, no word to say.
Our mouths feel foolish . . . For all the days hereafter
What have we saved--what news, what tune, what play?

'We see each other as vain and futile tricksters,--
Posturing like bald apes before a mirror;
No pity dims our eyes . . .
How many others, like ourselves, this instant,
See how the great world wizens, and are wise? . . .'

Well, you are right . . . No doubt, they fall, these seconds . . .
When suddenly all's distempered, vacuous, ugly,
And even those most like angels creep for schemes.
The one you love leans forward, smiles, deceives you,
Opens a door through which you see dark dreams.

But this is momentary . . . or else, enduring,
Leads you with devious eyes through mists and poisons
To horrible chaos, or suicide, or crime . . .
And all these others who at your conjuration
Grow pale, feeling the skeleton touch of time,--

Or, laughing sadly, talk of things important,
Or stare at mirrors, startled to see their faces,
Or drown in the waveless vacuum of their days,--
Suddenly, as from sleep, awake, forgetting
This nauseous dream; take up their accustomed ways,

Exhume the ghost of a joke, renew loud laughter,
Forget the moles above their sweethearts' eyebrows,
Lean to the music, rise,
And dance once more in a rose-festooned illusion
With kindness in their eyes . . .

They say (as we ourselves have said, remember)
'What wizardry this slow waltz works upon us!
And how it brings to mind forgotten things!'
They say 'How strange it is that one such evening
Can wake vague memories of so many springs!'

And so they go . . . In a thousand crowded places,
They sit to smile and talk, or rise to ragtime,
And, for their pleasures, agree or disagree.
With secret symbols they play on secret passions.
With cunning eyes they see

The innocent word that sets remembrance trembling,
The dubious word that sets the scared heart beating . . .
The pendulum on the wall
Shakes down seconds . . . They laugh at time, dissembling;
Or coil for a victim and do not talk at all.

X. LETTER

From time to time, lifting his eyes, he sees
The soft blue starlight through the one small window,
The moon above black trees, and clouds, and Venus,--
And turns to write . . . The clock, behind ticks softly.

It is so long, indeed, since I have written,--

Two years, almost, your last is turning yellow,--
That these first words I write seem cold and strange.
Are you the man I knew, or have you altered?
Altered, of course--just as I too have altered--
And whether towards each other, or more apart,
We cannot say . . . I've just re-read your letter--
Not through forgetfulness, but more for pleasure--

Pondering much on all you say in it
Of mystic consciousness--divine conversion--
The sense of oneness with the infinite,--
Faith in the world, its beauty, and its purpose . . .
Well, you believe one must have faith, in some sort,
If one's to talk through this dark world contented.
But is the world so dark? Or is it rather
Our own brute minds,--in which we hurry, trembling,
Through streets as yet unlighted? This, I think.

You have been always, let me say, "romantic,"--
Eager for color, for beauty, soon discontented
With a world of dust and stones and flesh too ailing:
Even before the question grew to problem
And drove you bickering into metaphysics,
You met on lower planes the same great dragon,
Seeking release, some fleeting satisfaction,
In strange aesthetics . . . You tried, as I remember,
One after one, strange cults, and some, too, morbid,
The cruder first, more violent sensations,
Gorgeously carnal things, conceived and acted
With splendid animal thirst . . . Then, by degrees,--
Savoring all more delicate gradations

In all that hue and tone may play on flesh,

Or thought on brain,--you passed, if I may say so,
From red and scarlet through morbid greens to mauve.
Let us regard ourselves, you used to say,
As instruments of music, whereon our lives
Will play as we desire: and let us yield
These subtle bodies and subtler brains and nerves
To all experience plays . . . And so you went
From subtle tune to subtler, each heard once,
Twice or thrice at the most, tiring of each;
And closing one by one your doors, drew in
Slowly, through darkening labyrinths of feeling,
Towards the central chamber . . . Which now you've reached.

What, then's, the secret of this ultimate chamber--
Or innermost, rather? If I see it clearly
It is the last, and cunningest, resort
Of one who has found this world of dust and flesh,--
This world of lamentations, death, injustice,
Sickness, humiliation, slow defeat,
Bareness, and ugliness, and iteration,--
Too meaningless; or, if it has a meaning,
Too tiresomely insistent on one meaning:

Futility . . . This world, I hear you saying,--
With lifted chin, and arm in outflung gesture,
Coldly imperious,--this transient world,
What has it then to give, if not containing
Deep hints of nobler worlds? We know its beauties,--
Momentary and trivial for the most part,
Perceived through flesh, passing like flesh away,--
And know how much outweighed they are by darkness.
We are like searchers in a house of darkness,
A house of dust; we creep with little lanterns,

Throwing our tremulous arcs of light at random,
Now here, now there, seeing a plane, an angle,
An edge, a curve, a wall, a broken stairway
Leading to who knows what; but never seeing
The whole at once . . . We grope our way a little,
And then grow tired. No matter what we touch,
Dust is the answer--dust: dust everywhere.
If this were all--what were the use, you ask?
But this is not: for why should we be seeking,
Why should we bring this need to seek for beauty,
To lift our minds, if there were only dust?
This is the central chamber you have come to:
Turning your back to the world, until you came
To this deep room, and looked through rose-stained windows,
And saw the hues of the world so sweetly changed.

Well, in a measure, so only do we all.
I am not sure that you can be refuted.
At the very last we all put faith in something,--
You in this ghost that animates your world,
This ethical ghost,--and I, you'll say, in reason,--
Or sensuous beauty,--or in my secret self . . .
Though as for that you put your faith in these,
As much as I do--and then, forsaking reason,--
Ascending, you would say, to intuition,--
You predicate this ghost of yours, as well.
Of course, you might have argued,--and you should have,--
That no such deep appearance of design
Could shape our world without entailing purpose:
For can design exist without a purpose?
Without conceiving mind? . . . We are like children
Who find, upon the sands, beside a sea,
Strange patterns drawn,--circles, arcs, ellipses,

Moulded in sand . . . Who put them there, we wonder?

Did someone draw them here before we came?
Or was it just the sea?--We pore upon them,
But find no answer--only suppositions.
And if these perfect shapes are evidence
Of immanent mind, it is but circumstantial:
We never come upon him at his work,
He never troubles us. He stands aloof--
Well, if he stands at all: is not concerned
With what we are or do. You, if you like,
May think he broods upon us, loves us, hates us,
Conceives some purpose of us. In so doing
You see, without much reason, will in law.
I am content to say, 'this world is ordered,
Happily so for us, by accident:
We go our ways untroubled save by laws
Of natural things.' Who makes the more assumption?

If we were wise--which God knows we are not--
(Notice I call on God!) we'd plumb this riddle
Not in the world we see, but in ourselves.
These brains of ours--these delicate spinal clusters--
Have limits: why not learn them, learn their cravings?
Which of the two minds, yours or mine, is sound?
Yours, which scorned the world that gave it freedom,
Until you managed to see that world as omen,--
Or mine, which likes the world, takes all for granted,
Sorrow as much as joy, and death as life?--
You lean on dreams, and take more credit for it.
I stand alone . . . Well, I take credit, too.
You find your pleasure in being at one with all things--
Fusing in lambent dream, rising and falling

As all things rise and fall . . . I do that too--
With reservations. I find more varied pleasure
In understanding: and so find beauty even
In this strange dream of yours you call the truth.

Well, I have bored you. And it's growing late.
For household news--what have you heard, I wonder?
You must have heard that Paul was dead, by this time--
Of spinal cancer. Nothing could be done--
We found it out too late. His death has changed me,
Deflected much of me that lived as he lived,
Saddened me, slowed me down. Such things will happen,
Life is composed of them; and it seems wisdom
To see them clearly, meditate upon them,
And understand what things flow out of them.
Otherwise, all goes on here much as always.
Why won't you come and see us, in the spring,
And bring old times with you?--If you could see me
Sitting here by the window, watching Venus
Go down behind my neighbor's poplar branches,--
Just where you used to sit,--I'm sure you'd come.
This year, they say, the springtime will be early.

XI. CONVERSATION: UNDERTONES

What shall we talk of? Li Po? Hokusai?
You narrow your long dark eyes to fascinate me;
You smile a little. . . . Outside, the night goes by.
I walk alone in a forest of ghostly trees . . .
Your pale hands rest palm downwards on your knees.

'These lines--converging, they suggest such distance!

The soul is drawn away, beyond horizons.
Lured out to what? One dares not think.
Sometimes, I glimpse these infinite perspectives
In intimate talk (with such as you) and shrink . . .

'One feels so petty!--One feels such--emptiness!--'
You mimic horror, let fall your lifted hand,
And smile at me; with brooding tenderness . . .
Alone on darkened waters I fall and rise;
Slow waves above me break, faint waves of cries.

'And then these colors . . . but who would dare describe them?
This faint rose-coral pink . . this green--pistachio?--
So insubstantial! Like the dim ghostly things
Two lovers find in love's still-twilight chambers . . .
Old peacock-fans, and fragrant silks, and rings . . .

'Rings, let us say, drawn from the hapless fingers
Of some great lady, many centuries nameless,--
Or is that too sepulchral?--dulled with dust;
And necklaces that crumble if you touch them;
And gold brocades that, breathed on, fall to rust.

'No--I am wrong . . . it is not these I sought for--!
Why did they come to mind? You understand me--
You know these strange vagaries of the brain!--'
--I walk alone in a forest of ghostly trees;
Your pale hands rest palm downwards on your knees;
These strange vagaries of yours are all too plain.

'But why perplex ourselves with tedious problems
Of art or . . . such things? . . . while we sit here, living,
With all that's in our secret hearts to say!--'

Hearts?--Your pale hand softly strokes the satin.
You play deep music--know well what you play.
You stroke the satin with thrilling of finger-tips,
You smile, with faintly perfumed lips,
You loose your thoughts like birds,
Brushing our dreams with soft and shadowy words . .
We know your words are foolish, yet sit here bound
In tremulous webs of sound.

'How beautiful is intimate talk like this!--
It is as if we dissolved grey walls between us,
Stepped through the solid portals, become but shadows,
To hear a hidden music . . . Our own vast shadows
Lean to a giant size on the windy walls,
Or dwindle away; we hear our soft footfalls
Echo forever behind us, ghostly clear,
Music sings far off, flows suddenly near,
And dies away like rain . . .
We walk through subterranean caves again,--
Vaguely above us feeling
A shadowy weight of frescos on the ceiling,
Strange half-lit things,
Soundless grotesques with writhing claws and wings . . .
And here a beautiful face looks down upon us;
And someone hurries before, unseen, and sings . . .
Have we seen all, I wonder, in these chambers--
Or is there yet some gorgeous vault, arched low,
Where sleeps an amazing beauty we do not know? . . '

The question falls: we walk in silence together,
Thinking of that deep vault and of its secret . . .
This lamp, these books, this fire
Are suddenly blown away in a whistling darkness.

Deep walls crash down in the whirlwind of desire.

XII. WITCHES' SABBATH

Now, when the moon slid under the cloud
And the cold clear dark of starlight fell,
He heard in his blood the well-known bell
Tolling slowly in heaves of sound,
Slowly beating, slowly beating,
Shaking its pulse on the stagnant air:
Sometimes it swung completely round,
Horribly gasping as if for breath;
Falling down with an anguished cry . . .
Now the red bat, he mused, will fly;
Something is marked, this night, for death . . .
And while he mused, along his blood
Flew ghostly voices, remote and thin,
They rose in the cavern of his brain,
Like ghosts they died away again;
And hands upon his heart were laid,
And music upon his flesh was played,
Until, as he was bidden to do,
He walked the wood he so well knew.
Through the cold dew he moved his feet,
And heard far off, as under the earth,
Discordant music in shuddering tones,
Screams of laughter, horrible mirth,
Clapping of hands, and thudding of drums,
And the long-drawn wail of one in pain.
To-night, he thought, I shall die again,
We shall die again in the red-eyed fire
To meet on the edge of the wood beyond

With the placid gaze of fed desire . . .
He walked; and behind the whisper of trees,
In and out, one walked with him:
She parted the branches and peered at him,
Through lowered lids her two eyes burned,
He heard her breath, he saw her hand,
Wherever he turned his way, she turned:
Kept pace with him, now fast, now slow;
Moving her white knees as he moved . . .
This is the one I have always loved;
This is the one whose bat-soul comes
To dance with me, flesh to flesh,
In the starlight dance of horns and drums . . .

The walls and roofs, the scarlet towers,
Sank down behind a rushing sky.
He heard a sweet song just begun
Abruptly shatter in tones and die.
It whirled away. Cold silence fell.
And again came tollings of a bell.

        *   *   *   *   *

This air is alive with witches: the white witch rides
Swifter than smoke on the starlit wind.
In the clear darkness, while the moon hides,
They come like dreams, like something remembered . .
Let us hurry! beloved; take my hand,
Forget these things that trouble your eyes,
Forget, forget! Our flesh is changed,
Lighter than smoke we wreathe and rise . . .

The cold air hisses between us . . . Beloved, beloved,

What was the word you said?
Something about clear music that sang through water . . .
I cannot remember. The storm-drops break on the leaves.
Something was lost in the darkness. Someone is dead.
Someone lies in the garden and grieves.
Look how the branches are tossed in this air,
Flinging their green to the earth!
Black clouds rush to devour the stars in the sky,
The moon stares down like a half-closed eye.
The leaves are scattered, the birds are blown,
Oaks crash down in the darkness,
We run from our windy shadows; we are running alone.

*   *   *   *   *

The moon was darkened: across it flew
The swift grey tenebrous shape he knew,
Like a thing of smoke it crossed the sky,
The witch! he said. And he heard a cry,
And another came, and another came,
And one, grown duskily red with blood,
Floated an instant across the moon,
Hung like a dull fantastic flame . . .
The earth has veins: they throb to-night,
The earth swells warm beneath my feet,
The tips of the trees grow red and bright,
The leaves are swollen, I feel them beat,
They press together, they push and sigh,
They listen to hear the great bat cry,
The great red bat with the woman's face . . .
Hurry! he said. And pace for pace
That other, who trod the dark with him,
Crushed the live leaves, reached out white hands

And closed her eyes, the better to see
The priests with claws, the lovers with hooves,
The fire-lit rock, the sarabands.
I am here! she said. The bough he broke--
Was it the snapping bough that spoke?
I am here! she said. The white thigh gleamed
Cold in starlight among dark leaves,
The head thrown backward as he had dreamed,
The shadowy red deep jasper mouth;
And the lifted hands, and the virgin breasts,
Passed beside him, and vanished away.
I am here! she cried. He answered 'Stay!'
And laughter arose, and near and far
Answering laughter rose and died . . .
Who is there? in the dark? he cried.
He stood in terror, and heard a sound
Of terrible hooves on the hollow ground;
They rushed, were still; a silence fell;
And he heard deep tollings of a bell.

*   *   *   *   *

Look beloved! Why do you hide your face?
Look, in the centre there, above the fire,
They are bearing the boy who blasphemed love!
They are playing a piercing music upon him
With a bow of living wire! . . .
The virgin harlot sings,
She leans above the beautiful anguished body,
And draws slow music from those strings.
They dance around him, they fling red roses upon him,
They trample him with their naked feet,
His cries are lost in laughter,

Their feet grow dark with his blood, they beat and
    beat,
They dance upon him, until he cries no more . . .
Have we not heard that cry before?
Somewhere, somewhere,
Beside a sea, in the green evening,
Beneath green clouds, in a copper sky . . .
Was it you? was it I?
They have quenched the fires, they dance in the darkness,
The satyrs have run among them to seize and tear,
Look! he has caught one by the hair,
She screams and falls, he bears her away with him,
And the night grows full of whistling wings.
Far off, one voice, serene and sweet,
Rises and sings . . .

'By the clear waters where once I died,
In the calm evening bright with stars. . . .'
Where have I heard these words? Was it you who sang them?
It was long ago.
Let us hurry, beloved! the hard hooves trample;
The treetops tremble and glow.

       *   *   *   *   *

In the clear dark, on silent wings,
The red bat hovers beneath her moon;
She drops through the fragrant night, and clings
Fast in the shadow, with hands like claws,
With soft eyes closed and mouth that feeds,
To the young white flesh that warmly bleeds.
The maidens circle in dance, and raise
From lifting throats, a soft-sung praise;

Their knees and breasts are white and bare,
They have hung pale roses in their hair,
Each of them as she dances by
Peers at the blood with a narrowed eye.
See how the red wing wraps him round,
See how the white youth struggles in vain!
The weak arms writhe in a soundless pain;
He writhes in the soft red veiny wings,
But still she whispers upon him and clings. . . .
This is the secret feast of love,
Look well, look well, before it dies,
See how the red one trembles above,
See how quiet the white one lies! . . . .

Wind through the trees. . . . and a voice is heard
Singing far off. The dead leaves fall. . . .
'By the clear waters where once I died,
In the calm evening bright with stars,
One among numberless avatars,
I wedded a mortal, a mortal bride,
And lay on the stones and gave my flesh,
And entered the hunger of him I loved.
How shall I ever escape this mesh
Or be from my lover's body removed?'
Dead leaves stream through the hurrying air
And the maenads dance with flying hair.

*   *   *   *   *

The priests with hooves, the lovers with horns,
Rise in the starlight, one by one,
They draw their knives on the spurting throats,
They smear the column with blood of goats,

They dabble the blood on hair and lips
And wait like stones for the moon's eclipse.
They stand like stones and stare at the sky
Where the moon leers down like a half-closed eye. . .
In the green moonlight still they stand
While wind flows over the darkened sand
And brood on the soft forgotten things
That filled their shadowy yesterdays. . . .
Where are the breasts, the scarlet wings? . . . .
They gaze at each other with troubled gaze. . . .
And then, as the shadow closes the moon,
Shout, and strike with their hooves the ground,
And rush through the dark, and fill the night
With a slowly dying clamor of sound.
There, where the great walls crowd the stars,
There, by the black wind-riven walls,
In a grove of twisted leafless trees. . . .
Who are these pilgrims, who are these,
These three, the one of whom stands upright,
While one lies weeping and one of them crawls?
The face that he turned was a wounded face,
I heard the dripping of blood on stones. . . .
Hooves had trampled and torn this place,
And the leaves were strewn with blood and bones.
Sometimes, I think, beneath my feet,
The warm earth stretches herself and sighs. . . .
Listen! I heard the slow heart beat. . . .
I will lie on this grass as a lover lies
And reach to the north and reach to the south
And seek in the darkness for her mouth.

*   *   *   *   *

Beloved, beloved, where the slow waves of the wind
Shatter pale foam among great trees,
Under the hurrying stars, under the heaving arches,
Like one whirled down under shadowy seas,
I run to find you, I run and cry,
Where are you? Where are you? It is I. It is I.
It is your eyes I seek, it is your windy hair,
Your starlight body that breathes in the darkness there.
Under the darkness I feel you stirring. . . .
Is this you? Is this you?
Bats in this air go whirring. . . .
And this soft mouth that darkly meets my mouth,
Is this the soft mouth I knew?
Darkness, and wind in the tortured trees;
And the patter of dew.

    *   *   *   *   *

Dance! Dance! Dance! Dance!
Dance till the brain is red with speed!
Dance till you fall! Lift your torches!
Kiss your lovers until they bleed!
Backward I draw your anguished hair
Until your eyes are stretched with pain;
Backward I press you until you cry,
Your lips grow white, I kiss you again,
I will take a torch and set you afire,
I will break your body and fling it away. . . .
Look, you are trembling. . . . Lie still, beloved!
Lock your hands in my hair, and say
Darling! darling! darling! darling!
All night long till the break of day.

Is it your heart I hear beneath me. . . .
Or the far tolling of that tower?
The voices are still that cried around us. . . .
The woods grow still for the sacred hour.
Rise, white lover! the day draws near.
The grey trees lean to the east in fear.
'By the clear waters where once I died . . . .'
Beloved, whose voice was this that cried?
'By the clear waters that reach the sun
By the clear waves that starward run. . . .
I found love's body and lost his soul,
And crumbled in flame that should have annealed. . .
How shall I ever again be whole,
By what dark waters shall I be healed?'

Silence. . . . the red leaves, one by one,
Fall. Far off, the maenads run.

Silence. Beneath my naked feet
The veins of the red earth swell and beat.
The dead leaves sigh on the troubled air,
Far off the maenads bind their hair. . . .
Hurry, beloved! the day comes soon.
The fire is drawn from the heart of the moon.

    *   *   *   *   *

The great bell cracks and falls at last.
The moon whirls out. The sky grows still.
Look, how the white cloud crosses the stars
And suddenly drops behind the hill!
Your eyes are placid, you smile at me,
We sit in the room by candle-light.

We peer in each other's veins and see
No sign of the things we saw this night.
Only, a song is in your ears,
A song you have heard, you think, in dream:
The song which only the demon hears,
In the dark forest where maenads scream . . .

'By the clear waters where once I died . . .
In the calm evening bright with stars . . . '
What do the strange words mean? you say,--
And touch my hand, and turn away.

XIII.

The half-shut doors through which we heard that music
Are softly closed. Horns mutter down to silence.
The stars whirl out, the night grows deep.
Darkness settles upon us. A vague refrain
Drowsily teases at the drowsy brain.
In numberless rooms we stretch ourselves and sleep.

Where have we been? What savage chaos of music
Whirls in our dreams?--We suddenly rise in darkness,
Open our eyes, cry out, and sleep once more.
We dream we are numberless sea-waves languidly foaming
A warm white moonlit shore;

Or clouds blown windily over a sky at midnight,
Or chords of music scattered in hurrying darkness,
Or a singing sound of rain . . .
We open our eyes and stare at the coiling darkness,
And enter our dreams again.

PART IV.

I. CLAIRVOYANT

'This envelope you say has something in it
Which once belonged to your dead son--or something
He knew, was fond of? Something he remembers?--
The soul flies far, and we can only call it
By things like these . . . a photograph, a letter,
Ribbon, or charm, or watch . . . '

. . . Wind flows softly, the long slow even wind,
Over the low roofs white with snow;
Wind blows, bearing cold clouds over the ocean,
One by one they melt and flow,--

Streaming one by one over trees and towers,
Coiling and gleaming in shafts of sun;
Wind flows, bearing clouds; the hurrying shadows
Flow under them one by one . . .

' . . . A spirit darkens before me . . . it is the spirit
Which in the flesh you called your son . . . A spirit
Young and strong and beautiful . . .

He says that he is happy, is much honored;
Forgives and is forgiven . . . rain and wind
Do not perplex him . . . storm and dust forgotten . .

The glittering wheels in wheels of time are broken
And laid aside . . . '

'Ask him why he did the thing he did!'

'He is unhappy. This thing, he says, transcends you:
Dust cannot hold what shines beyond the dust . . .
What seems calamity is less than a sigh;
What seems disgrace is nothing.'

'Ask him if the one he hurt is there,
And if she loves him still!'

'He tells you she is there, and loves him still,--
Not as she did, but as all spirits love . . .
A cloud of spirits has gathered about him.
They praise him and call him, they do him honor;
He is more beautiful, he shines upon them.'

. . . Wind flows softly, the long deep tremulous wind,
Over the low roofs white with snow . . .
Wind flows, bearing dreams; they gather and vanish,
One by one they sing and flow;

Over the outstretched lands of days remembered,
Over remembered tower and wall,
One by one they gather and talk in the darkness,
Rise and glimmer and fall . . .

'Ask him why he did the thing he did!
He knows I will understand!'

                    'It is too late:

He will not hear me: I have lost my power.'

'Three times I've asked him! He will never tell me.
God have mercy upon him. I will ask no more.'

II. DEATH: AND A DERISIVE CHORUS

The door is shut. She leaves the curtained office,
And down the grey-walled stairs comes trembling slowly
Towards the dazzling street.
Her withered hand clings tightly to the railing.
The long stairs rise and fall beneath her feet.

Here in the brilliant sun we jostle, waiting
To tear her secret out . . . We laugh, we hurry,
We go our way, revolving, sinister, slow.
She blinks in the sun, and then steps faintly downward.
We whirl her away, we shout, we spin, we flow.

Where have you been, old lady? We know your secret!--
Voices jangle about her, jeers, and laughter. . . .
She trembles, tries to hurry, averts her eyes.
Tell us the truth, old lady! where have you been?
She turns and turns, her brain grows dark with cries.

Look at the old fool tremble! She's been paying,--
Paying good money, too,--to talk to spirits. . . .
She thinks she's heard a message from one dead!
What did he tell you? Is he well and happy?
Don't lie to us--we all know what he said.

He said the one he murdered once still loves him;

He said the wheels in wheels of time are broken;
And dust and storm forgotten; and all forgiven. . . .
But what you asked he wouldn't tell you, though,--
Ha ha! there's one thing you will never know!
That's what you get for meddling so with heaven!

Where have you been, old lady? Where are you going?
We know, we know! She's been to gab with spirits.
Look at the old fool! getting ready to cry!
What have you got in an envelope, old lady?
A lock of hair? An eyelash from his eye?

How do you know the medium didn't fool you?
Perhaps he had no spirit--perhaps he killed it.
Here she comes! the old fool's lost her son.
What did he have--blue eyes and golden hair?
We know your secret! what's done is done.

Look out, you'll fall--and fall, if you're not careful,
Right into an open grave. . . but what's the hurry?
You don't think you will find him when you're dead?
Cry! Cry! Look at her mouth all twisted,--
Look at her eyes all red!

We know you--know your name and all about you,
All you remember and think, and all you scheme for.
We tear your secret out, we leave you, go
Laughingly down the street. . . . Die, if you want to!
Die, then, if you're in such a hurry to know!--

. . . . She falls. We lift her head. The wasted body
Weighs nothing in our hands. Does no one know her?
Was no one with her when she fell? . . .

We eddy about her, move away in silence.
We hear slow tollings of a bell.

III. PALIMPSEST: A DECEITFUL PORTRAIT

Well, as you say, we live for small horizons:
We move in crowds, we flow and talk together,
Seeing so many eyes and hands and faces,
So many mouths, and all with secret meanings,--
Yet know so little of them; only seeing
The small bright circle of our consciousness,
Beyond which lies the dark. Some few we know--
Or think we know. . . Once, on a sun-bright morning,
I walked in a certain hallway, trying to find
A certain door: I found one, tried it, opened,
And there in a spacious chamber, brightly lighted,
A hundred men played music, loudly, swiftly,
While one tall woman sent her voice above them
In powerful sweetness. . . . Closing then the door
I heard it die behind me, fade to whisper,--
And walked in a quiet hallway as before.
Just such a glimpse, as through that opened door,
Is all we know of those we call our friends. . . .
We hear a sudden music, see a playing
Of ordered thoughts--and all again is silence.
The music, we suppose, (as in ourselves)
Goes on forever there, behind shut doors,--
As it continues after our departure,
So, we divine, it played before we came . . .
What do you know of me, or I of you? . . .
Little enough. . . . We set these doors ajar
Only for chosen movements of the music:

This passage, (so I think--yet this is guesswork)
Will please him,--it is in a strain he fancies,--
More brilliant, though, than his; and while he likes it
He will be piqued . . . He looks at me bewildered
And thinks (to judge from self--this too is guesswork)

The music strangely subtle, deep in meaning,
Perplexed with implications; he suspects me
Of hidden riches, unexpected wisdom. . . .
Or else I let him hear a lyric passage,--
Simple and clear; and all the while he listens
I make pretence to think my doors are closed.
This too bewilders him. He eyes me sidelong
Wondering 'Is he such a fool as this?
Or only mocking?'--There I let it end. . . .
Sometimes, of course, and when we least suspect it--
When we pursue our thoughts with too much passion,
Talking with too great zeal--our doors fly open
Without intention; and the hungry watcher
Stares at the feast, carries away our secrets,
And laughs. . . . but this, for many counts, is seldom.
And for the most part we vouchsafe our friends,
Our lovers too, only such few clear notes
As we shall deem them likely to admire:
'Praise me for this' we say, or 'laugh at this,'
Or 'marvel at my candor'. . . . all the while
Withholding what's most precious to ourselves,--
Some sinister depth of lust or fear or hatred,
The sombre note that gives the chord its power;
Or a white loveliness--if such we know--
Too much like fire to speak of without shame.

Well, this being so, and we who know it being

So curious about those well-locked houses,
The minds of those we know,--to enter softly,
And steal from floor to floor up shadowy stairways,
From room to quiet room, from wall to wall,
Breathing deliberately the very air,
Pressing our hands and nerves against warm darkness
To learn what ghosts are there,--
Suppose for once I set my doors wide open
And bid you in. . . . Suppose I try to tell you
The secrets of this house, and how I live here;
Suppose I tell you who I am, in fact. . . .
Deceiving you--as far as I may know it--
Only so much as I deceive myself.

If you are clever you already see me
As one who moves forever in a cloud
Of warm bright vanity: a luminous cloud
Which falls on all things with a quivering magic,
Changing such outlines as a light may change,
Brightening what lies dark to me, concealing
Those things that will not change . . . I walk sustained
In a world of things that flatter me: a sky
Just as I would have had it; trees and grass
Just as I would have shaped and colored them;
Pigeons and clouds and sun and whirling shadows,
And stars that brightening climb through mist at nightfall,--
In some deep way I am aware these praise me:
Where they are beautiful, or hint of beauty,
They point, somehow, to me. . . . This water says,--
Shimmering at the sky, or undulating
In broken gleaming parodies of clouds,
Rippled in blue, or sending from cool depths
To meet the falling leaf the leaf's clear image,--

This water says, there is some secret in you
Akin to my clear beauty, silently responsive
To all that circles you. This bare tree says,--
Austere and stark and leafless, split with frost,
Resonant in the wind, with rigid branches
Flung out against the sky,--this tall tree says,
There is some cold austerity in you,
A frozen strength, with long roots gnarled on rocks,
Fertile and deep; you bide your time, are patient,
Serene in silence, bare to outward seeming,
Concealing what reserves of power and beauty!
What teeming Aprils!--chorus of leaves on leaves!
These houses say, such walls in walls as ours,
Such streets of walls, solid and smooth of surface,
Such hills and cities of walls, walls upon walls;
Motionless in the sun, or dark with rain;
Walls pierced with windows, where the light may enter;
Walls windowless where darkness is desired;
Towers and labyrinths and domes and chambers,--
Amazing deep recesses, dark on dark,--
All these are like the walls which shape your spirit:
You move, are warm, within them, laugh within them,
Proud of their depth and strength; or sally from them,
When you are bold, to blow great horns at the world. .
This deep cool room, with shadowed walls and ceiling,
Tranquil and cloistral, fragrant of my mind,
This cool room says,--just such a room have you,
It waits you always at the tops of stairways,
Withdrawn, remote, familiar to your uses,
Where you may cease pretence and be yourself. . . .
And this embroidery, hanging on this wall,
Hung there forever,--these so soundless glidings
Of dragons golden-scaled, sheer birds of azure,

Coilings of leaves in pale vermilion, griffins
Drawing their rainbow wings through involutions
Of mauve chrysanthemums and lotus flowers,--
This goblin wood where someone cries enchantment,--
This says, just such an involuted beauty
Of thought and coiling thought, dream linked with dream,
Image to image gliding, wreathing fires,
Soundlessly cries enchantment in your mind:
You need but sit and close your eyes a moment
To see these deep designs unfold themselves.

And so, all things discern me, name me, praise me--
I walk in a world of silent voices, praising;
And in this world you see me like a wraith
Blown softly here and there, on silent winds.
'Praise me'--I say; and look, not in a glass,
But in your eyes, to see my image there--
Or in your mind; you smile, I am contented;
You look at me, with interest unfeigned,
And listen--I am pleased; or else, alone,
I watch thin bubbles veering brightly upward
From unknown depths,--my silver thoughts ascending;
Saying now this, now that, hinting of all things,--
Dreams, and desires, velleities, regrets,
Faint ghosts of memory, strange recognitions,--
But all with one deep meaning: this is I,
This is the glistening secret holy I,
This silver-winged wonder, insubstantial,
This singing ghost. . . . And hearing, I am warmed.

*   *   *   *   *

You see me moving, then, as one who moves

Forever at the centre of his circle:
A circle filled with light. And into it
Come bulging shapes from darkness, loom gigantic,
Or huddle in dark again. . . . A clock ticks clearly,
A gas-jet steadily whirs, light streams across me;
Two church bells, with alternate beat, strike nine;
And through these things my pencil pushes softly
To weave grey webs of lines on this clear page.
Snow falls and melts; the eaves make liquid music;
Black wheel-tracks line the snow-touched street; I turn
And look one instant at the half-dark gardens,
Where skeleton elm-trees reach with frozen gesture
Above unsteady lamps,--with black boughs flung
Against a luminous snow-filled grey-gold sky.
'Beauty!' I cry. . . . My feet move on, and take me
Between dark walls, with orange squares for windows.
Beauty; beheld like someone half-forgotten,
Remembered, with slow pang, as one neglected . . .
Well, I am frustrate; life has beaten me,
The thing I strongly seized has turned to darkness,
And darkness rides my heart. . . . These skeleton elm-trees--
Leaning against that grey-gold snow filled sky--
Beauty! they say, and at the edge of darkness
Extend vain arms in a frozen gesture of protest . . .
A clock ticks softly; a gas-jet steadily whirs:
The pencil meets its shadow upon clear paper,
Voices are raised, a door is slammed. The lovers,
Murmuring in an adjacent room, grow silent,
The eaves make liquid music. . . . Hours have passed,
And nothing changes, and everything is changed.
Exultation is dead, Beauty is harlot,--
And walks the streets. The thing I strongly seized
Has turned to darkness, and darkness rides my heart.

If you could solve this darkness you would have me.
This causeless melancholy that comes with rain,
Or on such days as this when large wet snowflakes
Drop heavily, with rain . . . whence rises this?
Well, so-and-so, this morning when I saw him,
Seemed much preoccupied, and would not smile;
And you, I saw too much; and you, too little;
And the word I chose for you, the golden word,
The word that should have struck so deep in purpose,
And set so many doors of wish wide open,
You let it fall, and would not stoop for it,
And smiled at me, and would not let me guess
Whether you saw it fall. . . These things, together,
With other things, still slighter, wove to music,
And this in time drew up dark memories;
And there I stand. This music breaks and bleeds me,
Turning all frustrate dreams to chords and discords,
Faces and griefs, and words, and sunlit evenings,
And chains self-forged that will not break nor lengthen,
And cries that none can answer, few will hear.
Have these things meaning? Or would you see more clearly
If I should say 'My second wife grows tedious,
Or, like gay tulip, keeps no perfumed secret'?

Or 'one day dies eventless as another,
Leaving the seeker still unsatisfied,
And more convinced life yields no satisfaction'?
Or 'seek too hard, the sight at length grows callous,
And beauty shines in vain'?--

                    These things you ask for,
These you shall have. . . So, talking with my first wife,

At the dark end of evening, when she leaned
And smiled at me, with blue eyes weaving webs
Of finest fire, revolving me in scarlet,--
Calling to mind remote and small successions
Of countless other evenings ending so,--
I smiled, and met her kiss, and wished her dead;
Dead of a sudden sickness, or by my hands
Savagely killed; I saw her in her coffin,
I saw her coffin borne downstairs with trouble,
I saw myself alone there, palely watching,
Wearing a masque of grief so deeply acted
That grief itself possessed me. Time would pass,
And I should meet this girl,--my second wife--
And drop the masque of grief for one of passion.
Forward we move to meet, half hesitating,
We drown in each others' eyes, we laugh, we talk,
Looking now here, now there, faintly pretending
We do not hear the powerful pulsing prelude
Roaring beneath our words . . . The time approaches.
We lean unbalanced. The mute last glance between us,
Profoundly searching, opening, asking, yielding,
Is steadily met: our two lives draw together . . .
. . . .'What are you thinking of?'. . . . My first wife's voice
Scattered these ghosts. 'Oh nothing--nothing much--
Just wondering where we'd be two years from now,
And what we might be doing . . . ' And then remorse
Turned sharply in my mind to sudden pity,
And pity to echoed love. And one more evening
Drew to the usual end of sleep and silence.

And, as it is with this, so too with all things.
The pages of our lives are blurred palimpsest:
New lines are wreathed on old lines half-erased,

And those on older still; and so forever.
The old shines through the new, and colors it.
What's new? What's old? All things have double meanings,--
All things return. I write a line with passion
(Or touch a woman's hand, or plumb a doctrine)
Only to find the same thing, done before,--
Only to know the same thing comes to-morrow. . . .
This curious riddled dream I dreamed last night,--
Six years ago I dreamed it just as now;
The same man stooped to me; we rose from darkness,
And broke the accustomed order of our days,
And struck for the morning world, and warmth, and freedom. . . .
What does it mean? Why is this hint repeated?
What darkness does it spring from, seek to end?

You see me, then, pass up and down these stairways,
Now through a beam of light, and now through shadow,--
Pursuing silent ends. No rest there is,--
No more for me than you. I move here always,
From quiet room to room, from wall to wall,
Searching and plotting, weaving a web of days.
This is my house, and now, perhaps, you know me. . .
Yet I confess, for all my best intentions,
Once more I have deceived you. . . . I withhold
The one thing precious, the one dark thing that guides me;
And I have spread two snares for you, of lies.

IV. COUNTERPOINT: TWO ROOMS

He, in the room above, grown old and tired,
She, in the room below--his floor her ceiling--
Pursue their separate dreams. He turns his light,

And throws himself on the bed, face down, in laughter. . . .
She, by the window, smiles at a starlight night,

His watch--the same he has heard these cycles of ages--
Wearily chimes at seconds beneath his pillow.
The clock, upon her mantelpiece, strikes nine.
The night wears on. She hears dull steps above her.
The world whirs on. . . . New stars come up to shine.

His youth--far off--he sees it brightly walking
In a golden cloud. . . . Wings flashing about it. . . . Darkness
Walls it around with dripping enormous walls.
Old age--far off--her death--what do they matter?
Down the smooth purple night a streaked star falls.

She hears slow steps in the street--they chime like music;
They climb to her heart, they break and flower in beauty,
Along her veins they glisten and ring and burn. . . .
He hears his own slow steps tread down to silence.
Far off they pass. He knows they will never return.

Far off--on a smooth dark road--he hears them faintly.
The road, like a sombre river, quietly flowing,
Moves among murmurous walls. A deeper breath
Swells them to sound: he hears his steps more clearly.
And death seems nearer to him: or he to death.

What's death?--She smiles. The cool stone hurts her elbows.
The last of the rain-drops gather and fall from elm-boughs,
She sees them glisten and break. The arc-lamp sings,
The new leaves dip in the warm wet air and fragrance.
A sparrow whirs to the eaves, and shakes his wings.

What's death--what's death? The spring returns like music,
The trees are like dark lovers who dream in starlight,
The soft grey clouds go over the stars like dreams.
The cool stone wounds her arms to pain, to pleasure.
Under the lamp a circle of wet street gleams. . . .
And death seems far away, a thing of roses,
A golden portal, where golden music closes,
Death seems far away:
And spring returns, the countless singing of lovers,
And spring returns to stay. . . .

He, in the room above, grown old and tired,
Flings himself on the bed, face down, in laughter,
And clenches his hands, and remembers, and desires to die.
And she, by the window, smiles at a night of starlight.
. . . The soft grey clouds go slowly across the sky.

V. THE BITTER LOVE-SONG

No, I shall not say why it is that I love you--
Why do you ask me, save for vanity?
Surely you would not have me, like a mirror,
Say 'yes,--your hair curls darkly back from the temples,
Your mouth has a humorous, tremulous, half-shy sweetness,
Your eyes are April grey. . . . with jonquils in them?'
No, if I tell at all, I shall tell in silence . . .
I'll say--my childhood broke through chords of music
--Or were they chords of sun?--wherein fell shadows,
Or silences; I rose through seas of sunlight;
Or sometimes found a darkness stooped above me
With wings of death, and a face of cold clear beauty. .
I lay in the warm sweet grass on a blue May morning,

My chin in a dandelion, my hands in clover,
And drowsed there like a bee. . . . blue days behind me
Stretched like a chain of deep blue pools of magic,
Enchanted, silent, timeless. . . . days before me
Murmured of blue-sea mornings, noons of gold,
Green evenings streaked with lilac, bee-starred nights.
Confused soft clouds of music fled above me.

Sharp shafts of music dazzled my eyes and pierced me.
I ran and turned and spun and danced in the sunlight,
Shrank, sometimes, from the freezing silence of beauty,
Or crept once more to the warm white cave of sleep.

No, I shall not say 'this is why I praise you--
Because you say such wise things, or such foolish. . .'
You would not have me say what you know better?
Let me instead be silent, only saying--:
My childhood lives in me--or half-lives, rather--
And, if I close my eyes cool chords of music
Flow up to me . . . long chords of wind and sunlight. . . .
Shadows of intricate vines on sunlit walls,
Deep bells beating, with aeons of blue between them,
Grass blades leagues apart with worlds between them,
Walls rushing up to heaven with stars upon them. . .
I lay in my bed and through the tall night window
Saw the green lightning plunging among the clouds,
And heard the harsh rain storm at the panes and roof. . . .
How should I know--how should I now remember--
What half-dreamed great wings curved and sang above me?
What wings like swords? What eyes with the dread night in them?

This I shall say.--I lay by the hot white sand-dunes. .
Small yellow flowers, sapless and squat and spiny,

Stared at the sky. And silently there above us
Day after day, beyond our dreams and knowledge,
Presences swept, and over us streamed their shadows,
Swift and blue, or dark. . . . What did they mean?
What sinister threat of power? What hint of beauty?
Prelude to what gigantic music, or subtle?
Only I know these things leaned over me,
Brooded upon me, paused, went flowing softly,
Glided and passed. I loved, I desired, I hated,
I struggled, I yielded and loved, was warmed to blossom . . .
You, when your eyes have evening sunlight in them,
Set these dunes before me, these salt bright flowers,
These presences. . . . I drowse, they stream above me,
I struggle, I yield and love, I am warmed to dream.

You are the window (if I could tell I'd tell you)
Through which I see a clear far world of sunlight.
You are the silence (if you could hear you'd hear me)
In which I remember a thin still whisper of singing.
It is not you I laugh for, you I touch!
My hands, that touch you, suddenly touch white cobwebs,
Coldly silvered, heavily silvered with dewdrops;
And clover, heavy with rain; and cold green grass. . .

VI. CINEMA

As evening falls,
The walls grow luminous and warm, the walls
Tremble and glow with the lives within them moving,
Moving like music, secret and rich and warm.
How shall we live to-night, where shall we turn?
To what new light or darkness yearn?

A thousand winding stairs lead down before us;
And one by one in myriads we descend
By lamplit flowered walls, long balustrades,
Through half-lit halls which reach no end. . . .

Take my arm, then, you or you or you,
And let us walk abroad on the solid air:
Look how the organist's head, in silhouette,
Leans to the lamplit music's orange square! . . .
The dim-globed lamps illumine rows of faces,
Rows of hands and arms and hungry eyes,
They have hurried down from a myriad secret places,
From windy chambers next to the skies. . . .
The music comes upon us. . . . it shakes the darkness,
It shakes the darkness in our minds. . . .
And brilliant figures suddenly fill the darkness,
Down the white shaft of light they run through darkness,
And in our hearts a dazzling dream unwinds . . .

Take my hand, then, walk with me
By the slow soundless crashings of a sea
Down miles on miles of glistening mirrorlike sand,--
Take my hand
And walk with me once more by crumbling walls;
Up mouldering stairs where grey-stemmed ivy clings,
To hear forgotten bells, as evening falls,
Rippling above us invisibly their slowly widening rings. . . .
Did you once love me? Did you bear a name?
Did you once stand before me without shame? . . .
Take my hand: your face is one I know,
I loved you, long ago:
You are like music, long forgotten, suddenly come to mind;
You are like spring returned through snow.

Once, I know, I walked with you in starlight,
And many nights I slept and dreamed of you;
Come, let us climb once more these stairs of starlight,
This midnight stream of cloud-flung blue! . . .
Music murmurs beneath us like a sea,
And faints to a ghostly whisper . . . Come with me.

Are you still doubtful of me--hesitant still,
Fearful, perhaps, that I may yet remember
What you would gladly, if you could, forget?
You were unfaithful once, you met your lover;
Still in your heart you bear that red-eyed ember;
And I was silent,--you remember my silence yet . . .
You knew, as well as I, I could not kill him,
Nor touch him with hot hands, nor yet with hate.
No, and it was not you I saw with anger.
Instead, I rose and beat at steel-walled fate,
Cried till I lay exhausted, sick, unfriended,
That life, so seeming sure, and love, so certain,
Should loose such tricks, be so abruptly ended,
Ring down so suddenly an unlooked-for curtain.

How could I find it in my heart to hurt you,
You, whom this love could hurt much more than I?
No, you were pitiful, and I gave you pity;
And only hated you when I saw you cry.
We were two dupes; if I could give forgiveness,--
Had I the right,--I should forgive you now . . .
We were two dupes . . . Come, let us walk in starlight,
And feed our griefs: we do not break, but bow.

Take my hand, then, come with me
By the white shadowy crashings of a sea . . .

Look how the long volutes of foam unfold
To spread their mottled shimmer along the sand! . . .
Take my hand,
Do not remember how these depths are cold,
Nor how, when you are dead,
Green leagues of sea will glimmer above your head.
You lean your face upon your hands and cry,
The blown sand whispers about your feet,
Terrible seems it now to die,--
Terrible now, with life so incomplete,
To turn away from the balconies and the music,
The sunlit afternoons,
To hear behind you there a far-off laughter
Lost in a stirring of sand among dry dunes . . .
Die not sadly, you whom life has beaten!
Lift your face up, laughing, die like a queen!
Take cold flowers of foam in your warm white fingers!
Death's but a change of sky from blue to green . . .

As evening falls,
The walls grow luminous and warm, the walls
Tremble and glow . . . the music breathes upon us,
The rayed white shaft plays over our heads like magic,
And to and fro we move and lean and change . . .
You, in a world grown strange,
Laugh at a darkness, clench your hands despairing,
Smash your glass on a floor, no longer caring,
Sink suddenly down and cry . . .
You hear the applause that greets your latest rival,
You are forgotten: your rival--who knows?--is I . . .
I laugh in the warm bright light of answering laughter,
I am inspired and young . . . and though I see
You sitting alone there, dark, with shut eyes crying,

I bask in the light, and in your hate of me . . .
Failure . . . well, the time comes soon or later . . .
The night must come . . . and I'll be one who clings,
Desperately, to hold the applause, one instant,--
To keep some youngster waiting in the wings.

The music changes tone . . . a room is darkened,
Someone is moving . . . the crack of white light widens,
And all is dark again; till suddenly falls
A wandering disk of light on floor and walls,
Winks out, returns again, climbs and descends,
Gleams on a clock, a glass, shrinks back to darkness;
And then at last, in the chaos of that place,
Dazzles like frozen fire on your clear face.
Well, I have found you. We have met at last.
Now you shall not escape me: in your eyes
I see the horrible huddlings of your past,--
All you remember blackens, utters cries,
Reaches far hands and faint. I hold the light
Close to your cheek, watch the pained pupils shrink,--
Watch the vile ghosts of all you vilely think . . .
Now all the hatreds of my life have met
To hold high carnival . . . we do not speak,
My fingers find the well-loved throat they seek,
And press, and fling you down . . . and then forget.

Who plays for me? What sudden drums keep time
To the ecstatic rhythm of my crime?
What flute shrills out as moonlight strikes the floor? . .
What violin so faintly cries
Seeing how strangely in the moon he lies? . . .
The room grows dark once more,
The crack of white light narrows around the door,

And all is silent, except a slow complaining
Of flutes and violins, like music waning.

Take my hand, then, walk with me
By the slow soundless crashings of a sea . . .
Look, how white these shells are, on this sand!
Take my hand,
And watch the waves run inward from the sky
Line upon foaming line to plunge and die.
The music that bound our lives is lost behind us,
Paltry it seems . . . here in this wind-swung place
Motionless under the sky's vast vault of azure
We stand in a terror of beauty, face to face.
The dry grass creaks in the wind, the blown sand whispers,

The soft sand seethes on the dunes, the clear grains glisten,
Once they were rock . . . a chaos of golden boulders . . .
Now they are blown by the wind . . . we stand and listen
To the sliding of grain upon timeless grain
And feel our lives go past like a whisper of pain.
Have I not seen you, have we not met before
Here on this sun-and-sea-wrecked shore?
You shade your sea-gray eyes with a sunlit hand
And peer at me . . . far sea-gulls, in your eyes,
Flash in the sun, go down . . . I hear slow sand,
And shrink to nothing beneath blue brilliant skies . . .

    *   *   *   *   *

The music ends. The screen grows dark. We hurry
To go our devious secret ways, forgetting
Those many lives . . . We loved, we laughed, we killed,
We danced in fire, we drowned in a whirl of sea-waves.

The flutes are stilled, and a thousand dreams are stilled.

Whose body have I found beside dark waters,
The cold white body, garlanded with sea-weed?
Staring with wide eyes at the sky?
I bent my head above it, and cried in silence.
Only the things I dreamed of heard my cry.

Once I loved, and she I loved was darkened.
Again I loved, and love itself was darkened.
Vainly we follow the circle of shadowy days.
The screen at last grows dark, the flutes are silent.
The doors of night are closed. We go our ways.

VII.

The sun goes down in a cold pale flare of light.
The trees grow dark: the shadows lean to the east:
And lights wink out through the windows, one by one.
A clamor of frosty sirens mourns at the night.
Pale slate-grey clouds whirl up from the sunken sun.

And the wandering one, the inquisitive dreamer of dreams,
The eternal asker of answers, stands in the street,
And lifts his palms for the first cold ghost of rain.
The purple lights leap down the hill before him.
The gorgeous night has begun again.

'I will ask them all, I will ask them all their dreams,
I will hold my light above them and seek their faces,
I will hear them whisper, invisible in their veins. . . . '
The eternal asker of answers becomes as the darkness,

Or as a wind blown over a myriad forest,
Or as the numberless voices of long-drawn rains.

We hear him and take him among us like a wind of music,
Like the ghost of a music we have somewhere heard;
We crowd through the streets in a dazzle of pallid lamplight,
We pour in a sinister mass, we ascend a stair,
With laughter and cry, with word upon murmured word,
We flow, we descend, we turn. . . . and the eternal dreamer
Moves on among us like light, like evening air . . .

Good night! good night! good night! we go our ways,
The rain runs over the pavement before our feet,
The cold rain falls, the rain sings.
We walk, we run, we ride. We turn our faces
To what the eternal evening brings.

Our hands are hot and raw with the stones we have laid,
We have built a tower of stone high into the sky.
We have built a city of towers.
Our hands are light, they are singing with emptiness.
Our souls are light. They have shaken a burden of hours. . . .
What did we build it for? Was it all a dream? . . .
Ghostly above us in lamplight the towers gleam . . .
And after a while they will fall to dust and rain;
Or else we will tear them down with impatient hands;
And hew rock out of the earth, and build them again.

1916-1917

The Codes Of Hammurabi And Moses
W. W. Davies

QTY

The discovery of the Hammurabi Code is one of the greatest achievements of archaeology, and is of paramount interest, not only to the student of the Bible, but also to all those interested in ancient history...

Religion   **ISBN:** *1-59462-338-4*   **Pages:132**
MSRP $12.95

The Theory of Moral Sentiments
Adam Smith

QTY

This work from 1749. contains original theories of conscience amd moral judgment and it is the foundation for systemof morals.

Philosophy **ISBN:** *1-59462-777-0*   **Pages:536**
MSRP $19.95

Jessica's First Prayer
Hesba Stretton

QTY

In a screened and secluded corner of one of the many railway-bridges which span the streets of London there could be seen a few years ago, from five o'clock every morning until half past eight, a tidily set-out coffee-stall, consisting of a trestle and board, upon which stood two large tin cans, with a small fire of charcoal burning under each so as to keep the coffee boiling during the early hours of the morning when the work-people were thronging into the city on their way to their daily toil...

Pages:84

Childrens   **ISBN:** *1-59462-373-2*   **MSRP $9.95**

My Life and Work
Henry Ford

QTY

Henry Ford revolutionized the world with his implementation of mass production for the Model T automobile. Gain valuable business insight into his life and work with his own auto-biography... "We have only started on our development of our country we have not as yet, with all our talk of wonderful progress, done more than scratch the surface. The progress has been wonderful enough but..."

Pages:300

Biographies/   **ISBN:** *1-59462-198-5*   **MSRP $21.95**

The Art of Cross-Examination
Francis Wellman

QTY

I presume it is the experience of every author, after his first book is published upon an important subject, to be almost overwhelmed with a wealth of ideas and illustrations which could readily have been included in his book, and which to his own mind, at least, seem to make a second edition inevitable. Such certainly was the case with me; and when the first edition had reached its sixth impression in five months, I rejoiced to learn that it seemed to my publishers that the book had met with a sufficiently favorable reception to justify a second and considerably enlarged edition. ..

Reference   **ISBN:** *1-59462-647-2*

Pages:412

MSRP $19.95

On the Duty of Civil Disobedience
Henry David Thoreau

QTY

Thoreau wrote his famous essay, On the Duty of Civil Disobedience, as a protest against an unjust but popular war and the immoral but popular institution of slave-owning. He did more than write—he declined to pay his taxes, and was hauled off to gaol in consequence. Who can say how much this refusal of his hastened the end of the war and of slavery ?

Law   **ISBN:** *1-59462-747-9*   **Pages:48**

MSRP $7.45

Dream Psychology Psychoanalysis for Beginners
Sigmund Freud

QTY

Sigmund Freud, born Sigismund Schlomo Freud (May 6, 1856 - September 23, 1939), was a Jewish-Austrian neurologist and psychiatrist who co-founded the psychoanalytic school of psychology. Freud is best known for his theories of the unconscious mind, especially involving the mechanism of repression; his redefinition of sexual desire as mobile and directed towards a wide variety of objects; and his therapeutic techniques, especially his understanding of transference in the therapeutic relationship and the presumed value of dreams as sources of insight into unconscious desires.

Psychology   **ISBN:** *1-59462-905-6*

Pages:196

MSRP $15.45

The Miracle of Right Thought
Orison Swett Marden

QTY

Believe with all of your heart that you will do what you were made to do. When the mind has once formed the habit of holding cheerful, happy, prosperous pictures, it will not be easy to form the opposite habit. It does not matter how improbable or how far away this realization may see, or how dark the prospects may be, if we visualize them as best we can, as vividly as possible, hold tenaciously to them and vigorously struggle to attain them, they will gradually become actualized, realized in the life. But a desire, a longing without endeavor, a yearning abandoned or held indifferently will vanish without realization.

Pages:360

Self Help   **ISBN:** *1-59462-644-8*   *MSRP $25.45*

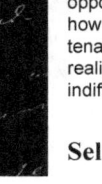

QTY

The Rosicrucian Cosmo-Conception Mystic Christianity *by Max Heindel*   ISBN: *1-59462-188-8* **$38.95**
The Rosicrucian Cosmo-conception is not dogmatic, neither does it appeal to any other authority than the reason of the student. It is: not controversial, but is: sent forth in the, hope that it may help to clear...   *New Age/Religion Pages 646*

Abandonment To Divine Providence *by Jean-Pierre de Caussade*   ISBN: *1-59462-228-0* **$25.95**
"The Rev. Jean Pierre de Caussade was one of the most remarkable spiritual writers of the Society of Jesus in France in the 18th Century. His death took place at Toulouse in 1751. His works have gone through many editions and have been republished...   *Inspirational/Religion Pages 400*

Mental Chemistry *by Charles Haanel*   ISBN: *1-59462-192-6* **$23.95**
Mental Chemistry allows the change of material conditions by combining and appropriately utilizing the power of the mind. Much like applied chemistry creates something new and unique out of careful combinations of chemicals the mastery of mental chemistry...   *New Age Pages 354*

The Letters of Robert Browning and Elizabeth Barret Barrett 1845-1846 vol II   ISBN: *1-59462-193-4* **$35.95**
by Robert Browning and Elizabeth Barrett   *Biographies Pages 596*

Gleanings In Genesis (volume I) *by Arthur W. Pink*   ISBN: *1-59462-130-6* **$27.45**
Appropriately has Genesis been termed "the seed plot of the Bible" for in it we have, in germ form, almost all of the great doctrines which are afterwards fully developed in the books of Scripture which follow...   *Religion/Inspirational Pages 420*

The Master Key *by L. W. de Laurence*   ISBN: *1-59462-001-6* **$30.95**
In no branch of human knowledge has there been a more lively increase of the spirit of research during the past few years than in the study of Psychology, Concentration and Mental Discipline. The requests for authentic lessons in Thought Control, Mental Discipline and...   New Age/Business Pages 422

The Lesser Key Of Solomon Goetia *by L. W. de Laurence*   ISBN: *1-59462-092-X* **$9.95**
This translation of the first book of the "Lernegton" which is now for the first time made accessible to students of Talismanic Magic was done, after careful collation and edition, from numerous Ancient Manuscripts in Hebrew, Latin, and French...   *New Age/Occult Pages 92*

Rubaiyat Of Omar Khayyam *by Edward Fitzgerald*   ISBN:*1-59462-332-5* **$13.95**
Edward Fitzgerald, whom the world has already learned, in spite of his own efforts to remain within the shadow of anonymity, to look upon as one of the rarest poets of the century, was born at Bredfield, in Suffolk, on the 31st of March, 1809. He was the third son of John Purcell...   *Music Pages 172*

Ancient Law *by Henry Maine*   ISBN: *1-59462-128-4* **$29.95**
The chief object of the following pages is to indicate some of the earliest ideas of mankind, as they are reflected in Ancient Law, and to point out the relation of those ideas to modern thought.   *Religion/History Pages 452*

Far-Away Stories *by William J. Locke*   ISBN: *1-59462-129-2* **$19.45**
"Good wine needs no bush, but a collection of mixed vintages does. And this book is just such a collection. Some of the stories I do not want to remain buried for ever in the museum files of dead magazine-numbers an author's not unpardonable vanity..."   *Fiction Pages 272*

Life of David Crockett *by David Crockett*   ISBN: *1-59462-250-7* **$27.45**
"Colonel David Crockett was one of the most remarkable men of the times in which he lived. Born in humble life, but gifted with a strong will, an indomitable courage, and unremitting perseverance...   *Biographies/New Age Pages 424*

Lip-Reading *by Edward Nitchie*   ISBN: *1-59462-206-X* **$25.95**
Edward B. Nitchie, founder of the New York School for the Hard of Hearing, now the Nitchie School of Lip-Reading, Inc, wrote "LIP-READING Principles and Practice". The development and perfecting of this meritorious work on lip-reading was an undertaking...   *How-to Pages 400*

A Handbook of Suggestive Therapeutics, Applied Hypnotism, Psychic Science   ISBN: *1-59462-214-0* **$24.95**
by Henry Munro   *Health/New Age/Health/Self-help Pages 376*

A Doll's House: and Two Other Plays *by Henrik Ibsen*   ISBN: *1-59462-112-8* **$19.95**
Henrik Ibsen created this classic when in revolutionary 1848 Rome. Introducing some striking concepts in playwriting for the realist genre, this play has been studied the world over.   *Fiction/Classics/Plays 308*

The Light of Asia *by sir Edwin Arnold*   ISBN: *1-59462-204-3* **$13.95**
In this poetic masterpiece, Edwin Arnold describes the life and teachings of Buddha. The man who was to become known as Buddha to the world was born as Prince Gautama of India but he rejected the worldly riches and abandoned the reigns of power when... Religion/History/Biographies Pages 170

The Complete Works of Guy de Maupassant *by Guy de Maupassant*   ISBN: *1-59462-157-8* **$16.95**
"For days and days, nights and nights, I had dreamed of that first kiss which was to consecrate our engagement, and I knew not on what spot I should put my lips..."   *Fiction/Classics Pages 240*

The Art of Cross-Examination *by Francis L. Wellman*   ISBN: *1-59462-309-0* **$26.95**
Written by a renowned trial lawyer, Wellman imparts his experience and uses case studies to explain how to use psychology to extract desired information through questioning.   *How-to/Science/Reference Pages 408*

Answered or Unanswered? *by Louisa Vaughan*   ISBN: *1-59462-248-5* **$10.95**
Miracles of Faith in China   *Religion Pages 112*

The Edinburgh Lectures on Mental Science (1909) *by Thomas*   ISBN: *1-59462-008-3* **$11.95**
This book contains the substance of a course of lectures recently given by the writer in the Queen Street Hall, Edinburgh. Its purpose is to indicate the Natural Principles governing the relation between Mental Action and Material Conditions...   *New Age/Psychology Pages 148*

Ayesha *by H. Rider Haggard*   ISBN: *1-59462-301-5* **$24.95**
Verily and indeed it is the unexpected that happens! Probably if there was one person upon the earth from whom the Editor of this, and of a certain previous history, did not expect to hear again...   *Classics Pages 380*

Ayala's Angel *by Anthony Trollope*   ISBN: *1-59462-352-X* **$29.95**
The two girls were both pretty, but Lucy who was twenty-one who supposed to be simple and comparatively unattractive, whereas Ayala was credited, as her Bombwhat romantic name might show, with poetic charm and a taste for romance. Ayala when her father died was nineteen...   *Fiction Pages 484*

The American Commonwealth *by James Bryce*   ISBN: *1-59462-286-8* **$34.45**
An interpretation of American democratic political theory. It examines political mechanics and society from the perspective of Scotsman James Bryce   *Politics Pages 572*

Stories of the Pilgrims *by Margaret P. Pumphrey*   ISBN: *1-59462-116-0* **$17.95**
This book explores pilgrims religious oppression in England as well as their escape to Holland and eventual crossing to America on the Mayflower, and their early days in New England...   *History Pages 268*

www.bookjungle.com *email: sales@bookjungle.com fax: 630-214-0564 mail: Book Jungle PO Box 2226 Champaign, IL 61825*

QTY

The Fasting Cure *by Sinclair Upton*   ISBN: *1-59462-222-1* **$13.95**

In the Cosmopolitan Magazine for May, 1910, and in the Contemporary Review (London, for April, 1910, I published an article dealing with my experi-ences in fasting. I have written a great many magazine articles, but never one which attracted so much attention... New Age/Self Help/Health Pages 164

Hebrew Astrology *by Sepharial*   ISBN: *1-59462-308-2* **$13.45**

In these days of advanced thinking it is a matter of common observation that we have left many of the old landmarks behind and that we are now pressing forward to greater heights and to a wider horizon than that which represented the mind-content of our progenitors... Astrology Pages 144

Thought Vibration or The Law of Attraction in the Thought World   ISBN: *1-59462-127-6* **$12.95**

by William Walker Atkinson   Psychology/Religion Pages 144

Optimism *by Helen Keller*   ISBN: *1-59462-108-X* **$15.95**

Helen Keller was blind, deaf, and mute since 19 months old, yet famously learned how to overcome these handicaps, communicate with the world, and spread her lectures promoting optimism. An inspiring read for everyone... Biographies/Inspirational Pages 84

Sara Crewe *by Frances Burnett*   ISBN: *1-59462-360-0*   **$9.45**

In the first place, Miss Minchin lived in London. Her home was a large, dull, tall one, in a large, dull square, where all the houses were alike, and all the sparrows were alike, and where all the door-knockers made the same heavy sound... Childrens/Classic Pages 88

The Autobiography of Benjamin Franklin *by Benjamin Franklin*   ISBN: *1-59462-135-7* **$24.95**

The Autobiography of Benjamin Franklin has probably been more extensively read than any other American historical work, and no other book of its kind has had such ups and downs of fortune. Franklin lived for many years in England, where he was agent... Biographies/History Pages 332

Name	
Email	
Telephone	
Address	
City, State ZIP	

☐ **Credit Card**   ☐ **Check / Money Order**

Credit Card Number	
Expiration Date	
Signature	

Please Mail to: Book Jungle
                   PO Box 2226
                   Champaign, IL 61825
or Fax to: 630-214-0564

ORDERING INFORMATION

web*: www.bookjungle.com*
email*: sales@bookjungle.com*
fax*: 630-214-0564*
mail*: Book Jungle PO Box 2226 Champaign, IL 61825*
or PayPal *to sales@bookjungle.com*

Please contact us for bulk discounts

DIRECT-ORDER TERMS

**20% Discount if You Order
Two or More Books**
Free Domestic Shipping!
Accepted: Master Card, Visa,
Discover, American Express

www.ingramcontent.com/pod-product-compliance
Lightning Source LLC
Chambersburg PA
CBHW082014170626
46817CB00009B/3099

* 9 7 8 1 4 3 8 5 1 7 4 4 5 *